Laid to Rest

by
E.F. Landeros

PublishAmerica
Baltimore

First printing

All characters in this book are fictitious, and any resemblance to real persons, living or dead, is coincidental.

PublishAmerica has allowed this work to remain exactly as the author intended, verbatim, without editorial input.

Hardcover 978-1-4489-3616-8
Softcover 978-1-4489-5090-4
PUBLISHED BY PUBLISHAMERICA, LLLP
www.publishamerica.com
Baltimore

Printed in the United States of America

As the clouds covered the sky, the wind started to howl between the trees.

What was it about this day that was like no other? Where were the blocked thoughts that had once overpowered the very existence of my brain stems? And why am I so cold? Why has the sounds of nature stopped abruptly in the middle of the afternoon? Why am I so COLD!? These thoughts and more carried themselves along my mind. Here I was a well-known author of many other books. Yet, here I stood in the doorway of the cabin overlooking the lake, wondering why my last book wouldn't drive itself from my minds eye and onto the computer that sat in the living room. The answer I already knew.

As I stood there, I saw in the distance over the lake the moon and sun side by side as it usually is in the middle of the day, and the sky was clear. I thought to myself, "*How can it be that one great and marvelous star can shine its brightest, and yet still the glory of the dim rock and ice can also be seen?* "*Yet very faintly it could be made out to the grand shape that it holds.* Then, I thought about myself. "*Here I stand at the brightest time in my career and yet the public can see my dark side, the troubles and the anger, the fame and the love, the romance and the literature.*"*All these in which were taking their toll on this author of mystery.*

I couldn't bear to look at the outside anymore, the scene that had talked to me no longer was in my interest. What I was interested in was to get this book finished. It had stirred up so much commotion with my loved ones and the ones that were there for me. I needed this book out on paper and away from the desk where it dwelled for months.

Why can't it just leave! Why am I having so much trouble? Whereas, in the past, when paper and pen were set in front of my face, I could write down novels upon novels of murder, deceit, love, and lies. Where was the young man that I once knew? The man who would call the people he loved and tell them that this book was dedicated to them for they are the ones who needed to get away from the world? Why!? Why can't someone write a book for me for a change? Don't they know that an author needs to get away too!? I HATE IT!

My mind was now going to overflow and I felt as if all the worries were going to spill out on the floor in front of me. It should have. I was feeling as if the cold hand of despair was taking a hold of my lungs and clenching them as tight as one hundred turns to a vice.

I didn't usually ask myself so many questions, nor did I ever need any of them answered, but life had changed since I had moved to this lake. What I do not understand is what I am going to do now. How will my story end? What will the readers say? Will I go down in history among the other writers before me? I just seemed to keep questioning myself.

Hours had past, and I was indeed ready for a rest. The moon had now taken its place in the sky among the billions of stars, a giant sphere shining over the quiet and caressing black blanket of nightfall. Once again I familiarized myself with this space occupant. There I was in the dark, still an author, shining over the other authors of the past. Their thoughts weren't as bright as mine. Mine were brighter, and I shone over them, I told myself that I knew the truth. As a person with dreams, your hope for yourself is to exceed your own expectations. I knew though that my light was really brought on by another source. I was shone because I had stolen my light.

Bedtime didn't come as easy as it usually did for me, because my conscience was finally catching up to me, The thing that I had kept to myself had finally been clawing it's way in the corner of my mind, Even though I had given a human characteristic to this matter it really felt as if it was piercing the back of my head and howling to be released from my memory one way or another. I took a muscle relaxer and went to bed.

It was Monday morning and I had just gotten off the phone with my editor. "This is your last book Edward; you need to show the readers what they want! You need to go out with a boom! You need to finish before the deadline!" That was just like Lily. She would always tell me something that I wanted to hear but only followed by something I didn't want to hear.

"What am I to do, Lily?" I asked her with some hope that she would have a logical answer. "Today is Monday and the book has to be finished by Friday. You expect me to finish this book in LESS THAN SEVEN DAYS?" Her answer was quicker than her last, "Yes, Ed. You need to get this done by Friday or else you just have to fall back on your last book as your final masterpiece..." Knowing that my last book wasn't really that great of an effort on my point, I got a little edgy." I am not going to let you do this to me anymore, Lily. You're always making my decisions and always making these deadlines which are always impossible to keep!" And with that I hung up the phone.

From the day she took John's place as my editor I didn't like her. As for John, now that was an editor! He would always let me know things ahead of time and was also around the same age as I was. We were known as the Senior Sellers of Marble Page Publishing. Now that John retired, I got stuck with Lily; 20 years younger than me but very good with helping me find words to work with. I told her once that she should write a book along side with me and then we could compare thoughts. She wasn't into any of that. Editing was her second profession. Her first had something to do with cosmetology school or something. She said," I just came to work here because I wanted to be closer to the well known author of Mystery!!! ED!!!"

I got up from my table and went for the stack of papers in my office. "Where is it?" I looked for the manila folder that held my rough draft to my book. I finally found it shoved underneath the bills of debt that I had received from the electric company, my cell phone provider along with the numerous letters from loyal readers of my literature and then the occasional hate letter, of the woman who tells me that my book reminds me too much of her life and that I am onto her and blah blah blah... But there it was my last "Masterpiece" as John called it, clasped shut and ready to be tended to yet again....But not ready to be tended to by me.

As I reached the front door I felt to myself an uneasiness, hopelessness for the task set before me. How was I supposed to get this book done in less than a week, whereas my last titles had taken me months to complete...and sometimes years? But however I was going to do it, I needed to get away from this office, I needed to travel to the city and finish my book.

It has been ten years since I have spoken of her... too long or just too soon I am not sure. I don't know if I want to, but now it is time for me to speak...It has come to my attention that she does not want to stay trapped inside my memory any longer....

Her name was and is Edith Merrill. She was my Ghostwriter, The people loved her work but the credit was stolen, sited by the greedy hands & life of Edward Larson. Me. She wasn't the one to complain or to worry about the literature that had to be done, for her stories were told long before they hit paper. They left her lips and hit the vast oxygen that had surrounded her and laid to rest in my brain. She always made sure that I knew what she wanted written and didn't let me question the outcome of her latest thoughts... and I never did ... until now.

I stood at the Bart Station in Daly City, San Francisco. Down there you will find your mass majority of people your lawyers, artist, poets, and your usual pan handlers. I feel the claustrophobia closing in and around my body. *Why am I here among these people?* I began to wonder. *Are they watching me?* Here

I am, clouding my mind with thoughts. *Haight and Ashbury....why was I going there?*

The air from the tunnel glided out like a blast of cool, yet sea breezed atom bomb of wind. The bright lights of the Bart shone luminously, blinding my pupils making it hard for me to read the route number on the side. The intercom came on relieving the fear of my chance of getting on the wrong route and therefore to the wrong location. I wasn't necessarily going to get off at Haight and Ashbury. I was on my way there on the number forty-three and was starting my tour of the city, or so I thought.

I picked a seat near a window, one that was facing backwards so that it would feel as if I was going backwards. They say that if you walk ten feet forward and then ten feet back you will see where you have been and by choosing this spot I felt as if I could go back in time. The smell around me was fairly clean although I did know that I wasn't the first or the last person to be sitting in this Bart car. From my briefcase I pulled out some gum to chew to ease the pain of the air pockets in my ears. Then pulled out some scratch paper and began to write.

Ghostwritten by Edward Larson
There she is the ghost of my memories running after me in an array of hazy colors,
Smiling at me I know she will have her revenge.
Her cold, icy dead hand bellowing in the wind and reaching out for my sanity,
When will she stop this madness of her own glory?
When we she dwell in another place, no longer causing my writing to be slander smitten?
When will I write and her stories be ghostwritten?

With those very words I wondered, *"Why am I letting her control my life still?" She's gone! Move on old man! Forgive and forget because your time is coming soon.* "What a horrible thing to think about but the truth of the matter is I am seventy years old and have been in bad shape for awhile now. The end will soon be near for me. The car I was sitting in stopped and let more passengers in. A couple in their early twenties sat across from me. I took a glimpse up from my paper and went back down memory lane to Nineteen fifty-five, when I first met Edith. Oh, what a glorious night that was. The night everything changed. And when I say everything, I MEAN EVERYTHING!!!

The moon was just closing in on the crystal clear water of Emerald Lake. It was named for the green willow that grew out of the middle of the lake. When hit by moonlight and at just the right angle would bring a Emerald glow to the fresh water waves caused by the breeze of a cool summer night.

"Edward," she said, "Peter and Allison said that if I walked down to the lake I would find a young man down here with the same interest as mine."

I was sitting in a fold up chair next to a card table with a pile of paper and a typewriter, "Go away!." I said "Let me be! and tell them that I am tired of them making fun of me and when my books are on the shelves then they will have their last laughs!" I was so frustrated. Peter was my high school buddy and Allison, his sweetheart, were very nice and timid teens, but into a lot of partying and alcohol Me on the other hand, I was going to be a writer. I was not your regular sort of teen.

"What are you writing there?" I heard her ask curiously.

"I am trying to write! I need quiet! If you want to just stand down here and make fun of me then just do it and go along, I do not have time for this jester of my work. I am just trying to have fun like you guys are, just in my own way!" I knew I was being a little harsh but I was really tired of their harassment and their laughter saying that I thought I was going to be the next big thing.

"Fun, who said I was making fun or even had any attention of doing so? And that is fun to me. I am a writer too you know?" She said with a little hurt sound in her voice and with that I turned around.

There in front of me, was this girl. She was about a few inches shorter than me. With moonlight in her eyes, this added superior, but yet not much needed enhancement on her already beautiful honey dipped hazel eyes. Her hair lay softly against her skin. When she saw that I was dumbfounded she looked to the ground.

"I am sorry to bother you, I am just going to go now." she said hesitantly.

"There is no need to go anywhere Miss; I didn't mean to startle you with my anger." I replied, very sorry for my first impression. "Here!" I continued. "Here grab a seat." I was hoping she would take me up on my offer.
"If you insist. I won't be any bother to you I hope." She said, as she reluctantly sat down.
"I am writing about how this lake makes me feel, and the

emotion I feel just being here in it's presence." I said, trying not to sound corny.

"So let's hear it!" With the sound in her voice, I wondered if she really was interested or was she still putting on a show brought forth by my old buddy and pal Peter.

Hesitant, I started to look down at my paper. The emptiness stared right back at me as if I were holding a ghostly masterpiece of which only I could see. If I could only write down what I saw, the feeling of embarrassment wouldn't have come over me with such a sudden rush of clammy hands and hard breathing.

"Uhhh....I uh..." I was trying to force out the words that so hardly taunted my mind with uncertain extent. *What was I to say?*

"You don't have anything do you?" The sound of her voice was very sad and I could feel her hurt.

"I see what I want to write but I don't ever get what I want down on paper! My stories and poems are trapped within the great iron bars of my mind and no matter how hard I try they just will not rid themselves from my mind!." I couldn't believe that I had just told her what had been confusing me forever. The simple but confusing reason I could not write.

"Here let me try to help you!" Her thoughtfulness intrigued me and I just waited for what she would say next.
"You want to help me? No one has ever offered to help me just ridicule my phantom ness of literature." Sadly I knew this was the truth.

"Well then you could call me your Ghostwriter. My name is Edith Merrill." She said stretching out a sideways hand. "And you are?"

I wondered if I should tell her my real name. I wanted to come up with a good one like William Poe, or Shakespeare Dickinson, but those names were already taken and so I was left alone with the name that I was given. The name that gave me infamous popularity when I accidentally burned down the old school house and the local paper read, **"Larson the Arson"**.

"My name is Edward Larson." I finally agreed with myself to say and returned the hand gesture clasping my hand around hers. Oh how soft it was! How it made me feel at ease as if her hands were like a cloud. I could tell that her fingertips were a little rougher than the rest positively showing that she had typed a thing or two in her young life.

"Well then Edward; let's see what our minds can do." She started brainstorming ideas to start the poem and I would give her the next line on down and so on and so forth and by the end of two hours It was finished.

"Now, let's start that over again." Pausing a moment and then as if the last two hours were just déjà vous she said. "So let's hear it."

This time, when I looked down the writing that had once been trapped was lying to rest on the clean white blanket of paper. Which was still able to be seen, but yet was being protected by this poem:

Emeralds' Essence
The water moves so softly upon the bank of the lake,
A sway ward wave of the branches on the weeper the wind does make,
The moons reflection shows its giant glow,
As it passes the leaves and makes a Emerald flow,
My worries are no longer mine to dwell,
For upon this lake my love calmly fell,
For I knew love and beauty ever since,
I caught a glimpse of Emeralds Essence.

I couldn't believe that this person that shared this view with me had seen or known what I wanted to express. *Why was it that she had this thing about her that reminded me of a figment of my own imagination?* She had to be. How else would she have been able to see into my imagination?

"Excuse me sir?" an unfamiliar voice said. "Sir?" I shook my head and focused on the person addressing me.

In front of me sat this different couple. One very muscular and covered in tattoo's with a earring in his left ear. The other one was very slender and very oddly dressed with a red dress and some very hairy legs that were very manly which went so perfectly with the woman's voice. *We must have hit Castro Street,* I thought for these were definitely homosexuals. Castro Theatre was known as a very unique theatre which would always feature a look at that side of sexuality.

"Do we like, know you from somewhere." said the red dressed one.

"You look very familiar." said the other

I wasn't sure what I wanted to say. Actually I was very sure of what I wanted to say I wanted to say no. Not because of the fact that they were homosexual men. It was the fact that I really did not want these people to know who I was because the truth of the matter was I did not know who I had become. I really didn't want the spotlight put on me in a very public place.

"I don't know who I am." I said shaking the truth a bit.

"Oh, I totally understand I have been through that too!" said the drag queen. "Once I tried to change my name to..."

His or her words (whatever they wanted to be) brought back yet another thought of a time with Edith when he said "Change my name."

It was five months after that night that I met Edith that she came up with her bright plan. What she had in mind this morning gave me a premonition that things weren't going to settle well in our relationship. If we became angered at each other, the truth might hurt or even destroy us.

"You know that poem that you wrote awhile back?" She said, with a voice that told me she was up to something.

"You mean the one we wrote together?" I replied not wanting to take credit for the whole piece.
"Yeah, well I think you should send it in to a person that publishes beginners in poetry and literature." Her words started to sink in.

"But that wouldn't be fair since you helped me a lot with the construction of that piece." I said yet again not wanting to take all the credit.

"Since your guilt trip here is not a good start for an inspiring writer than we can help you feel less guilty." Yet again, I knew she had a plan

And so it began. Edith Merrill became my Ghostwriter. The definition of a Ghostwriter, in my profession is a person that writes for you, but let's you get credit for their work. I did not want it this way it was just the way it turned out! I mean, without her I could not write. Without her ideas and thoughts my words wouldn't have ever came out of there captive state. Edith said that if the name at the end of all my writings and than later all my books would say "Ed" that way it could have a meaning of both Ed...ward Larson and Ed...ith Merrill. I took out the paper from the night on the lake sat it on the table and with a few pen strokes I added:

I caught a glimpse of Emerald's Essence.

By ED And with that I sent it off to the first publishing company in the book Marble Page Publishing. And so my poem collection was started.

Three mornings later Edith arrived at my house with a stack of envelopes in her hands. She rang on the doorbell and stood there humming very loudly. It was a tune that I recognized, but ignored because of how early the hour was. It was only six in the morning!

"Good Morning Edward!" She cheerfully said as she handed me the stack of envelopes.

"What are these?" I said very confused. *Why was she there so early and why had she given me a stack of envelopes?*

"Your mail silly, man your mailman comes early!"

"He doesn't," I thought of saying." I just didn't check the mail yesterday." But instead I smiled.

"Well then what are you waiting for? I see that you got something from M.P Publishing." She said pretending I didn't see it on the top of the pile.

"Yes, I see that! I wonder what it says." Turning it over I had seen that the side of it was already precisely cut.

"You know that it is a federal offense to open someone else's mail, don't you!" I said, not angrily but stating facts.

"I am sorry but I just wanted to know what it said! Come on read it." She said sounding very anxious.

So I took up the courage pulled the neatly folded paper out of its package and began to scan line to line.

Dear Mr. ED,
I am pleased to inform you that my staff and I here at M.P. Publishing have been very grateful to have read your piece titled Emerald's Essence. This penmanship has a lot of descriptive and

breathtaking detail which almost makes you feel as if you are at the scene. We are happy that we have become acquainted with you and we wish to hear more from you. Please let us be the first to know of your newest work. We will be keeping your present poem on hand to add to a collector's book.

Thanks again for choosing us!
Colin Louvaille
M.P CEO

I couldn't believe the words that I had just read; somebody was actually interested in my work. Well our work. And next to the paper folded neatly in half was a Post–It note attached to a one hundred dollar bill which read: *"To buy all the supplies you need for your next masterpiece."* That was one of the most wonderful experiences that I had .Yet, I still felt guilty of conjuring up all this excitement and leaving Edith in the shadows.

"Wow this is GREAT!" I smiled and hugged Edith, which she returned in my favor whole heartedly.

"So what do you say, we take that money go get some paper and ink and stuff and get started." She said already stoked to go.

"Yeah, let's do it! What do I have to lose? I wasn't expecting a weekend like this!" I went upstairs changed and headed out the door.

As we slowly came to another stop I wondered. *Where I am I headed?* I knew that Haight and Ashbury was my final destination. *But, where was I headed until then and why was I going there again?* I knew that I had to spend about a week in Frisco. *Why did I pick today to go to Haight and Ashbury?* I knew there wasn't a reason. I just had this unsubtle feeling that it was where I was suppose to end my day at. I don't know if it was my seat or if it was me but I could have sworn we were going back in time because that couple was there sitting in front of me. Not the ones from Castro street, but that young couple that reminded me of Edith and I.

"So where do you want to go and eat?" The young man asked the girl next to him.

"I don't know. Anywhere you want to go is fine with me." She answered him cheerfully.

I could tell that this was either their first week together or within their first months because if a woman is asked where she wants to eat or where she wants to go there is *no* doubt her mind where she wants to go. She already had the destination picked before she answered him with that lovable answer. She just wanted him to believe that he was in control of the day, but I knew by the sound and look in her eyes she was going to have her way no matter what. I am not saying anything negative of the female population, but they are tricky like that.

"Uhh, I don't know. What are you hungry for," said the man again putting the decision on her.

"Well, how about Chinese you do like Chinese don't you?" So cunningly did she sneak that one in there.

I knew it! I knew she was going to have her way! I thought there is no outsmarting this old man. I mean in my seventy years of life I had been around the block a time or two I knew the tricks and the moves that woman make even so did I know the steps that us men take also. I was not surprised at all with the young man's reply.

"Yeah, that sounds pretty good," he told her.

Not wanting to hurt her feelings or to prove her wrong is why this man did that. I knew by his face he was no fan of the oriental cuisine. This conversation, yet again, took me back to the first night Edith and I worked together as writing companions and also became companions in the making.

All that writing was going to pay off sooner than we thought. Two months later and we were getting close to a new beginning for ourselves. We were at the table in my cabin on Emerald Lake.

The cold air outside was whistling through the frozen willow. We could hear the branches break and hit the iced over water below. When I was outside I could see the fish and the lake weeds all frozen in one place as they were when the temperature dropped. It was crazy how at one second they were going along with there busy day going here and going there and then all of a sudden silence...no movement...No worries. How I wish that the moment Edith and I were at the table would have frozen also but it seemed that the only thing that was burning cold was our tempers.

"That is not the way that it is suppose to happen!" She would say after each line that I would write.

"Well Miss Smarty-Pants how would you describe it?" The question arose from my mouth with each repeating statement.

"First of all, she should be very eager of wanting him to hold her." She finally replied after the thousandth time.

"Oh yeah, well he's probably just waiting for her to show him some kind of emotion showing that she is interested." I fought back.

"What can't he see it in her eyes? I mean he is right there in front of her. Can't he see she needs him?" she was confused.

We had been working for the last six hours on the ending of our first book. A *Warm Winter Walk* and we were getting to the part where the main characters were finding out they were falling in love. Edith couldn't go with my, he is waiting for her to make the first move, and I couldn't go with her everything has to be according to the books story. I knew right then I wanted to hold her in my arms and sit by the fire huddled in a blanket just listening to the snow nestle on the windows of the house. I think she knew it too. We didn't say much after that except for I love you. We left the table, away from the book and like the fish in the lake, we took our place in the living room and spent the rest of the night in the arms of each other in a passionate embrace we stayed for the night.

"These gas prices are ridiculous' No wonder everyone is riding the Bart these days." A man said to his newly acquaintance.

"Yeah bro, I know but it is funny how no matter how high it gets we still buy it," said the man next to him.

I was watching them in the reflection of the window. I could see that the man who had just gotten on looked very high class with his hair whitened with the stress that his law office had given him. The other man was short and had black slicked back hair, white shirt and black aviator sunglasses which reflected the collection of gold chains that hung around his neck. He also had a scar on his hand. When he took off his sunglasses the faded out black tattoo under his eye showed meaning to the man's attire. *It is crazy.* I thought. *How all these different sorts of people can live in the same world. The high class and the low class and yet there are some matters that can bring the two together such as gas had done to these to young men.*

I started to look away from the window and then I saw a reflection that made the hair on the back of my neck turn on end. My blood ran cold and my eyes widened to the shock that was placed in front of me. It was her. It was Edith. There she was, staring at me. She had switch spots with the shorter guy and she glanced back at my reflection as I did to hers. Now this would have brought me joy and excitement before. Oh how I loved it when I saw her, but there was something that just wasn't right with this picture. I wanted to scream instead of smile with joy. Edith couldn't have been behind me because Edith was dead!

"NO!" I got up out of my seat and headed for the doors not looking back.

The whole density of it all was too much for me to handle. I couldn't get myself to look back. I was not ready to stand face to face with her again. Our last conversation did not end out well. I could feel her eyes their dead white filled glare staring at me in my brain. *How could it be? I know that she died! I know that she was gone or at least I thought she was gone. She had been dead for ten years.*

Standing outside at a Bart Station, I was wondering if what I had just seen was real or imaginary. *You know with me being a writer and all, I could just blow it off as a over reacted thought, right?* The air was cold around me now. I could see the fog start to come in off the bay. It's slow and dimmed homecoming pacing it's way in my direction...you got to be kidding me. First I see my Edith who has been dead for a decade now and than the fog rolls in my way. *Can this day get any creepier?*

* * * * *

"So do you want to write a horror story?" Edith asked me with excitement.

When asking a question like that, she would be really saying "Our next book is going to be a horror story."

25

Looking into her eyes I could see the story already taking place in front of me like a motion picture. Edith had a way of telling you a story. It would come to life right in front of your face. The problem with her new idea was that all horror stories are the same they are either unreal or they are too real you can't believe them. I mean look at it this way, a giant fly coming from Outer space attacking the very lives of a quiet sleepy town, or a series of murders in a small town happens and the people of the town are all suspects? Living in a small town growing up, I could see that really happening. How gossip spreads with everyone knowing everyone.

"So what do you think Ed?" her voice seeping through my thoughts.

"Uh sure, why not?" I said knowing that if I hadn't agreed my life would be a horror story.

"Okay, okay! Soooo....the main character is in this town and fog rolls in...." she started.

* * * * *

Pacing my way to a short little restaurant on the corner of I don't know, I think to myself I hope my day doesn't end like Mr. Cole's. He was our main character in our book *In the Tick of Night,* In which Mr. Cole's faces a fog that carries a deadly unknown secret. *Oh man I really hope that doesn't happen to me. I know that my imagination is taking a rather interesting toll on me and I think it's time for a rest.*
As I walk into this restaurant a man comes up to me and leads me to a seat in the corner of the darkened room. The lights were

26

dim and the whole area around me smelled of the musk of sea men and the salty smell of seawater. The air drifted through cracks in the walls and the paint was tattered here and there. I sat down into the bench seated booth and looked up at the waiter.

The man stood about six foot. He had a long gray beard, many wrinkles lapped over more wrinkles on his face. His skin texture was leathery looking due to the many years working in this restaurant I assumed.

"Welcome to Captains Corner. My name is Harold what can I git yer?" he talked down to me his breath reeked of tuna and lemon juice.

Not wanting to smell his breath, I looked down at my menu. The piece of paper was yellowed with age and tattered like the paint that decorated the restaurants interior. I could only make out a few things on it which read: Chips and Red Wine.

"Uh, do you have any Coke?." I was hoping at least that was on there even though the menu looked as if it was from the eighteen hundreds.

"Aye, Matey we got whats yer lookin fer," he answered me in a pirate's voice. He turned and went into the double doors which read "The Slop Room".

As I looked around me I saw the other occupants in the room. By their looks and the smells that lingered around me I could see why the man named Harold talked like a pirate. I couldn't imagine what it was that held these men to their fish and chips, but than once again, this was San Francisco. In Frisco you could be the Freak of Frisco and everyone would just look at you and walk right by.

"Here ya go!" Harold came back with a tall glass as yellow as the menu.

"Thanks, how much do I owe you?" I asked.

"Oh yer don't owe me nuttin, it's on dee house." He said with a yellowed smile. I thought to myself, the theme of this restaurant must be yellow.

"Thanks." I was surprised.

"No problem, Larson the Arson," and with that he walked away.

I looked down at my Coke I was waiting so long for a taste of its refreshing texture, but the ice that floated in the dark elixir made me ill. It seems that Harold left a few beard hairs in the ice machine. *How can this be? How can I see Edith and then when I want to get my mind off of those things I don't even get that?* A getaway I guess was not in my book I thought. Little did I know that would all change.

"How can you live this way?" Edith was complaining while she was walking around my apartment picking up a shirt and shoes.

"I don't know, I guess I didn't have reason to clean because the only person to see my apartment is me!" I snapped.

Edith had moved in with me a few months after the night that we spent together. Edith had the tendency to change my exterior and interior motives when it came to my house. When Edith came into my life, she not only took control of my literature, she became in control of everything from the roof to the floor and from one wall to another. When she slept, I slept and when she woke up at two in the morning with a new idea for a book, I was up also.

I couldn't believe that we had gotten married two months ago and now she was Edith Larson. That helped when we would publish a book with the pen name Ed Larson. She was my bride and I was her husband and good income came in and we lived well in our little house on Mitron Blvd, We lived well for the time being...

When I left Captain's Corner, the fog had with no matter of a doubt darkened the once opaque but cracked windows. I did not know where I was or where I was headed, due to the fact that I had left the Bart train and ran quite a long while. I was scared out of my mind. The cool mist sprayed my face as I walked down a long wooden walkway. *Why would I think of such a horrid thing of seeing Edith in such a real shape and form as I had? Do I remember why I was here? Oh, yes now I remember. I need to go to Haight and Ashbury. Now if I could only find out where I am."* All these thoughts were making me nauseated. I didn't know whether or not it was the thoughts or it was all the running I had done.

It was not long after I had asked myself these questions that I ran into a sign. Looking up, I squinted to make out the word. Since the fog eased down a bit I could actually see my feet again it read. PIER 39. I must have gotten off at The Embarcadero and ended up here by some chance. The wind was picking up a little and blowing my black P-coat back. It was not a rainy day, I just knew that it would get really cold if I kept my travels close to the bay and not closer in land. I did not get to have my refreshing glass of Coke thanks to Harold's shedding, but there was another refreshment on my mind and that was a cappuccino from Ghirardelli Square.

* * * * *

"Are you almost ready?" I heard her call from downstairs.

This was the fifth time in the last five minutes she had asked me that same question.

"Almost. You wanted me to wear the navy blue shirt remember? Have to find it."

"How come every time we have something important to do you take your sweet little time?"

I did not understand what she was talking about. I was ready three hours ago, but she had to do her hair.

"I'll be down there in a minute hon; I think I know where it is"

I didn't really know where it could have been, but that would probably keep her off my back for a few seconds.

"We'll the convention starts at seven and it's five o' clock right now!"

That was Edith. We had been to twenty-five of these annual conventions and every time she wanted to be the first one there.

I finally found the stupid shirt and put it on. Forty-six years old and I was still wearing that stupid navy blue button up. I wore it every year since the first convention.

As we drove down Mitron I looked over at Edith in her elegant black lace dress with an even darker slip underneath. I saw her hair starting to gray but still as beautiful as a fall walnut. A light lip gloss bringing out the shine to her pearly white teeth. She looked as though she were going to a funeral. I tried to keep my mind on the road, but the aggravation of thinking of her whispering my speech behind my back was gut twisting. There she was in her prime, with her jewelry and her top notch dress that I had just bought her yesterday. There I was with my dyed black hair covering the blanket of pepper my head now gave home to and my navy FADED blue shirt with a button missing on the right sleeve. Oh, this night was going to be different. I didn't know why and I didn't know how, but this night I was going to go against my dearest Edith....and I liked it.

I decided not to get back on the Bart again because the thought of seeing Edith again. I didn't want to succumb to any of the thoughts that she brought forth when I did see her. I walked away from Pier 39 and the "yellow" restaurant and made my way down to Grant Avenue. As I walked by the Grant and Green bar I could smell the strong stench of liquor that filled the air. I had never been much of a drinker, but Edith on the other hand on some occasions that was her oxygen. This trip to the city had already become a race against time, my book! *What about my book? How am I going to get it finished?*

The convention hall was filled with the miraculous glow of three grand chandeliers all in a row above the twenty tables and the one hundred chairs. There was little stage set up front with two golden statues on either side of the stage. The statues showed the figures of two people standing and reading a book. One of a man and the other a woman. Two arches ran from the statues head. They met together in a half hearted shape. The middle of the heart pointed down to the cherry-walnut podium where the speaker was to stand. The meaning of this decor was to show that the person in the middle made up what the others were reading.

As I made my way down the middle of the room I looked at the tables all vacant except the five wine glasses and a folded piece of white paper placed in the middle. Each of them were painted with bold and italic lettering naming who was suppose to sit at each table and what book they were going to be rewarded for. I glanced down at each table on the right hand side of the room for that is where all the authors from MP Publishing sat and I read each card:

J. Genton—Confessions of the Dark
W. Thomas—Silent Symphonies

I do not know what had made me look the other way. Something told me to turn around, and so I did. There on the table I looked at the piece of paper, and I got an uneasy feeling You see at this convention we get rewarded for our books and our efforts. Out of the twenty-five that I have been to, this was the first time I had seen this name:

P.H. and A. McKey—Inferno of Intelligence

I turned to Edith to tell her what I had seen, but she was already talking to him. He stood about a half a foot shorter than her. He had a white Ronald Reagan hairstyle and glasses with a golden rim. He stood there with his wife and another young woman that I did not know. When I looked at this man's eyes, I knew without a minute of doubt this was my friend Peter McKey

I finally made it down North Point Street in a cab and was now sitting at the Mermaid Fountain within the vicinity of Ghirardelli Square. I was sipping on my mocha cappuccino and staring out towards the statues in the middle of the water and that is when I thought to myself I wish I had a child. The mermaids in the middle of the fountain are holding their babies, and that was the moment I felt alone. I was without a child to love, to hold, to bring up and to show this world to and to enjoy all the fun things that the world had to offer. Like the playgrounds and the museums, the foods and the movies. The hurt deep inside was far greater than I could describe on paper. Tears came to my eyes as I, for a second, no longer thought of my book, or the past. Instead I sat there and I daydreamed of what it would have been like to hold a child in my arms and tell them I was their father.

"Oh man, how and when did you get into the writing business?" I was so astonished that my best friend had shared my interest.

"Edward, you inspired me to write. Once I saw how well Edith and you got along together doing such a thing I had too." that was his answer? He started writing when he saw the relationship between Edith and I? Oh, what a poor man to be contradicted by his assumptions.

I turned my attention to the lady next to him who I recognized to be Allison Warner.

"What about you Ally, how do you feel about Peter's writing accomplishments?" I wondered what interest she had in his works.

"Oh, I am very pleased with our work," she replied.

"Our works?, what do you mean?." I was confused by her response.

"Peter and I work on our books together and take great pride in our works." she said happily.

When she had said that, I felt guilt. I also felt uneasiness in my throat. *What was I feeling sorry for? Edith got credit, not that it was highly publicized or not publicized at all but...*I could feel Edith looking at me. I didn't have to turn around to feel it. I knew what she was thinking and I knew that about this time the exclusion of my earnings were taking their toll upon her. I needed and wanted to change the subject quickly and so I turned to the other young girl with Peter and Ally.

Shaking her hand nervously still feeling the wrath of Edith's stare I said "Hello, I don't think we have met. My name is Edward Larson."
The young girl with walnut brown hair and hazel eyes looked at me and smiled. "Pleased to meet you Mr. Larson I have heard a lot about you."

"Oh, you have? That is wonderful!" This was great a young reader of my works here at a convention to maybe someday idolize me?

"Yes, Mr. Larson, dad has told me great things about his best friend."

"Oh, Peter and Allison this is your daughter what a grand surprise!" I was shocked that they had a child for they were more of an independent couple.

Peter answered my astonishment "Yeah Ed, this is Melissa. She heard so much about you and didn't want to stay at home for this convention."

They went and took their seats on the left and we went to the right. Our small conversation must have took awhile because more people came walking in.

First came Janet Genton and her family and then came John over to my table along with Mr. Louvaille. Everyone seemed to be there but there was one empty chair.

"Why is that chair empty?" I started to get aggravated. My table shouldn't have one more chair and it definitely shouldn't have been empty.

"UH EXCUSE ME." I hollered at the passing waiter. "There is an extra chair at this table and there are only four of us." I wanted it gone.

Just then Melissa came over to our table and asked if she could sit down.

"I am sorry to bother you Mr. Larson, but Dad's table doesn't have a chair for me and he told me to come and ask you if I could join your table"

I usually would not allow other rivals to dine with me, but this was my best friend's daughter and she liked my work and so I let her stay.

"Welcome all to the While I was Writing Convention of Nineteen—ninety four. Tonight we are pleased to announce we have a new writer at this convention.

Doctor Peter McKey and his wife Allison, who have written their first non-fiction, book *Inferno of Intelligence* their book is based on..."

Man, she bored me to death. Why didn't she ever let us tell what our book was about?, she would always start out, " This is Edward Larson and his book was about a man and woman who don't understand what is wrong with their house because things keep getting moved around and disappearing and they believe that there is a supernatural force going about their home. In real life it was just a burglar all along." She wouldn't actually tell the whole story, but she might as well have as she goes on and on about it." I shook the thoughts and returned to listening to her.

"The names of the people in this book are changed, but the facts are real," and then she stopped talking.

Edith, Melissa, John and Colin were looking at me, but I didn't understand the meaning of their stares. It was as if they wanted me to say something. I guess it was just my imagination because they returned their gazes to the stage. On stage now, was Walter Thomas talking about the silver screen before sound. Silent movies bugged me so I didn't listen to Walter either.

"Mr. Larson are you going to come up on stage, or do you want to do your speech from there?" Melissa asked.

"Oh is it my turn? Alright let's do this." I adjusted the earpiece in my ear that Edith had bought me awhile back for this occasion. Edith took her seat behind me up on stage and she must have done a very great ventriloquist act because no one ever seemed to notice that she was talking.

I knew she was drunk because by this time she had to have had nineteen glasses of wine because she would refill after each speech.

"Good evening everyone." she said through the earphone in my ear.

"Good evening everyone... "I mimicked.

"First of all I would like to thank all of you for coming out this evening to be rewarded."

Again I mimicked her words.

"I would like to thank M.P. Publishing for giving my work a chance those twenty six years ago."

Again I repeated her words.
"I would also like to thank my editor John Pricter for editing my work and fixing my mistakes," Edith whispered.

"I would also like to thank John Pricter for, what do you do again?" John laughed.

I couldn't have the other writers know that I make mistakes on spelling and punctuation; I wanted them to adore me, not shun me.

"You selfish man, you take pride in our work; at least give this man the recognition he deserves! You always take and take but never return."

I did not want to hear myself get degraded in such a way so I took the headphone out of my ear and finished the speech myself.

Twenty minutes later I finished with, "And that is how my idea was laid to rest on the pages of your memory."

When the convention was over and done with, I said my farewells to the McKeys and Edith and I got into our car and drove home. The trip home was the quietist it had been in a long time. I hadn't heard that much silence from her side of the car since she went to go stay with her mother in seventy-one. Needless to say I did not write a book that year, nor did I want to.

That was the year that I instead went and bought Emerald Lake and had the construction of a cabin put there right next to the spot where Edith and I had first met. This was going to be our new home. We were going to move out of the small apartment that we were now living in.

Edith didn't seem happy to have a new cabin when she got back from her mother's. She said it was because of some fight she had with her mother and for quite some time afterwards she was very upset, but things came around and she forgot the fight with her mother and she was happy to be home on Emerald Lake.

I got up from the fountain, finishing my cappuccino and decided that it was time for me explore. My body now full of caffeine I knew I would have the energy to walk around the whole city it felt like. The fog had showed up again and as I started to walk away from the fountain. I heard someone call my name as I turned around I saw her, Edith sitting on the opposite side of the fountain. I dropped my cup and ran.

Exhausted, I decided that I no longer wanted to run or walk, since I had just seen "Edith" in Ghirardelli Square; *She definitely wouldn't be on the Bart right?* I tried to calm myself down and ease myself to get back on the Bart and ride around in it for awhile until my heart rate cooled down, or dead people stopped following me.

Once again down in the Bart terminal this time I did not have to wait for my train to show up, due to the fact that I was not headed in a certain direction this time. That's right Haight and Ashbury could wait. I couldn't believe of all the running I did that day, I mean I was in pretty good shape, other than the fact that I was seventy-years old and it must have looked funny to the onlookers that a man of my age would be scared of something so much that he would run around the city.

When I was seated, this time facing the opposite direction and seated away from the window. I knew that I might have seemed a bit paranoid but the truth was just that I was paranoid, scared, worried, and tired all at once. A man sat down next to me and he had in his hand a book Its cover was quite familiar to me for the fact that I wrote it.

"You must read this book sir, it's quite absurd this one is, it makes no sense." His words ate away at my patience.

"I have read it, and I think it makes PERFECT sense." This man did not know what he was talking about. That book was the last book I had written so far.

"No, how could a main character love a person so much but not give them the gratitude they deserved?" he was angry about this book, I could tell.

"Maybe he did love her but she was going to tell his secrets. He couldn't have that." I said reassuring that the book was plain to understand.

"You think that is why this author did so badly on this book? Because people hated the main character so much they hated the book." his words were right.

"GET AWAY from me," I was so angered at his last comment I wanted to strangle the man to death.

Edith didn't talk to me for a long time after the convention, she was so angry of the exclusion that I had with my thankfulness to John. Time did heal the scars of anger and once again she and I were back in the swing of things, with the late night writing and the scheduling of book signings and balancing of the checkbook and then it came the letter that changed the whole route of the way Edith and I saw each other, a milestone that would change the rest of our lives.

Dear Mr. Larson,

I am deeply saddened to inform you that Colin Louvaille passed away this Tuesday and has given you along with John Pricter ownership of Marble Page Publishing, It is noted that you also are allowed to inherit the remaining amount of two-hundred thousand dollars in which you are to split in half with Mr. Pricter, I am sorry to have had to bring you this news and in such an informal way but this is how Mr. Louvaille wanted it, in writing as he wanted all of his business done.

Mr. Andy Jenkins Lawyer for Louvaille

I put the letter down on the table, not wanting to show it to Edith. I wondered if I should just burn it so that the evidence was gone. I couldn't let Edith see the letter but I couldn't really explain how I became control of M.P. Publishing and I certainly wouldn't be able to cover the fact that Colin died.

I decided to confront her that night with the contents of that letter that I held so tightly in my hand. I was going to let her know what I planned to do with that large amount of sum that I had now been gifted with.

I found Edith in the bedroom on the computer. She was typing something and when she saw my presence, she clicked off the document she had been typing but in my favor she didn't do that gesture before saving her project.

"Honey, there is something that I have to tell you." I hated having to tell Edith things that she did not know.
I knew that she could tell by the sound of my voice and the look on my face that it was important.

"What is it, Ed?" The look of worry fell upon her face.

"Colin...died and he left me a letter." I tried not to smile.

"But..." She started to get a sick look on her face and the color left her once peach cheeks.

"I know honey."These things happen." I tried to comfort her.

"No, Ed, these things just don't happen. There are reasons people die. They're sick or they are killed. There is something behind Colin's death."

In the last forty years of our marriage, Edith hadn't ever referred to Colin as Colin, I didn't start calling him Colin until a few years back but remembering what I had seen not long before, reminded me of why should would call him by such an informal name.

      * * * * *

If this man knew what was good for him, he would shut up. I knew by the way that he was talking that he either did not know who I was or he really wanted to piss me off.

The view of the scenery went by in a blur and my ears started hurting. I didn't know if it was the pressure that the motion was giving them, or it was the on and on ranting of the jackass next to me.

The Bart came to a halt and the lights went out.

"Oh, great," the man said, "here comes Michael Myers."

Even though I was extremely mad at the man, I knew he was right. It seemed as if we were in the middle of a horror flick. The lights gave a flicker or two now and then, making me wonder if they were going to come back on. Looking at those lights made me think of myself when I was shining and making a living, and now I am old and flickering out.

"I hope he has something to eat, because I am starving," the man chuckled for a second.

I was just about to laugh at the man's last comment but I got interrupted by the brush of the man getting up and I heard him walk away.

"Excuse me, sir?" I started searching around the air around me, trying to find him.

The Bart was pitch black now and not a sound could be heard from a mile away.

"Why did you call him Colin?" I wanted to know if she would tell me the real reason she gave him such an informal address.

"What can't I call him Colin?" She was amazed at my concern.
"You can; it's just in forty years you've called him Mr. Louvaille." I still knew something was up.

"Anyways..." I said changing the subject but not forgetting.

"Anyways...What?" Edith's voice was tense.

"M.P. Publishing is now owned by yours truly."

"He left the company all to you?" she sounded like she was surprised. Colin and I had been friends for years why wouldn't he?

"Well, yes, and John Pricter," I said under my breath.

"Now that you have that responsibility I wonder if now you will treat him fairly."

"That brings me to subject number two..." I didn't know if I wanted to tell her due to the content of her last comment.

"What else is it, Edward?" Her anger was definitely showing and I knew that she was disgusted by me.

"I am now in the possession of two hundred thousand dollars." I was waiting for her to strike. I knew she was going to have something to say; she always did have something to say at a time like this. What I did not know is that I really didn't want to hear what she had to say this time.

The temperature in the Bart started to drop. The heat was off and it was the middle of November. I closed my eyes, trying not to think of what could be in my surroundings. Basically I was hoping to God that Edith wouldn't be sitting next to me when I opened my eyes.

My mind drifted off into a dream where the light came back on and Edith was sitting next to me waving her finger at me." Now you've done it, Ed. You've gotten rid of the people who mattered to you most, ha, I forgot. It was never the people who mattered to you, It was your books. You are your own worst enemy, Edward Larson...You hear me? You are going to be the cause of your own destruction.

"No!" The beads of sweat had returned to my forehead and my palms were clammy.

"What's wrong, sir?" asked the man next to me.

"Nothing....it's in the past." I muttered

Even in my sleep, I was not safe from my conscience or from Edith Merrill. She would always seem to follow me.

* * * * *

"I know Ed," her words were soft but yet they shocked me as if I was in the spot of a cheating husband.

"What do you mean' you know?" *This woman really did keep things hidden from me and I felt sorry for having to tell her Colin died?*

"Last year Colin told me that he was soon going to retire." her voice starting to tremble as though she stood face to face with a killer.

"He told me to take over M.P. Publishing. I resigned from the offer and instead told him to pick you and John." Her words seeped into my blood, setting it on fire

"The bastard was going to leave the company to you!? "And He didn't tell me? Why that two timing son of a..."

"Wait," she said, "There is more." She became uneasy. "I made a deal with him."

I wish she would have stopped at the part where she told Colin to pick John and I for the owner position but she had to go on to tell me that the two hundred thousand was out of my bank account and it was her way of paying John back for all that he had done for me and what I had put him through, since it was such a small amount she did not think that I was going to miss it. I would get half back, but the other fifty percent of it would go to John for his mental distress that I supposedly had brought upon him.

Word by word, it pierced my heart that Edith would turn on my like that. I was going to forgive her because I did understand her point of view on the subject matter, but she didn't stop there. She didn't keep her mouth closed! She SHOULD have been silent but....NO!

"Haight and Ashbury; I need to get to Haight and Ashbury." I kept repeating to myself.

The cell phone rang and I reached in my coat and grabbed it. I looked at the caller ID I got nervous when I saw the name **Lily Delano.** She probably wanted to know why it was taking me so long to get back to town.

Why couldn't I have ever just lived in peace with Edith, given the credit where credit was due? I did not want to answer this call, nor did I care what she was going to say since it would probably just consist of her telling me that I only had a few days left before the deadline. She got worried because I hadn't called her, and if I was a great author like I said I was I would keep in touch with my editor. I decided that even though I had the premonition of what she would say, I should just answer the cell to see if I was right. And so I put it to my ear.

"Hello?" that sounded pretty dumb but what else was I to say?

"Ed, it's Lily....where are you?" Her voice sounded a little angry.

"I'm in San Francisco and as we speak I am on the Bart." I wondered why she asked me that she had already known where I was I told her yesterday.

"Ok, I need you to get off and meet me at the Sir Francis Drake Hotel; I will be in the lobby waiting for you." She sounded excited.

"Uh, ok I guess I will meet you there then." I was surprised that she was in San Francisco and that she wanted to visit with me.

"Good, do you have your book done yet?" I knew that was going to be part of the conversation.

"I have about half of the book done." I guess she was surprised to hear that since I had only been gone for about four days.

"Good, so I could see the manuscript then and edit it." Even though I didn't know what to say I agreed and cut off connection with Lily.

You are probably wondering how in the world did I get half a book done in four days? Well it's as simple as this. Edith taught me that what you really should do in order to get a book done really fast is to not worry about the spelling or the punctuation and just write down whatever comes to your head, don't worry about how it comes out, just bring a story to your head and make it up as you go along write it down. Worry about placement and punctuation later.

* * * * *

The anger in the room was growing very tense between Edith and I. I really couldn't believe that she would do this to me. I wanted to know what was going on between her and Colin Louvaille but when I kept asking her, she would say it was nothing for me to worry about.

"What deal did you make with him, Edith Larson? Tell me I want to know!" I didn't really want to know but it ate away at me inside.

"Fine! You want to know Edward!? You want to know what I have been working on when you are away doing your book signings?"

I couldn't believe there was actually something going on and what I was about to see was going to send me over the edge. I walked towards the computer where she motioned me to come and I looked over her shoulder while she opened up a text document which was called **In His Shadow**. As I read down the page my anger was rushing fast like a fall wind blowing hard against the colorful trees, except in my mind was the view of crimson leaves, I saw red. I bet at that moment the tears that I would have cried would have looked like blood if they were colored the same as the anger I was feeling. There, in front of me was Edith's tell all book. She was going to let our secret that I had her write most of my stories. What was I going to do? My whole fame was going to end because of the thoughtless act of this woman. I looked behind me to the trophy from last years convention I read the gold writing it read: **Edward Larson, Author of Awe.**

"I'm sorry Ed, I couldn't live with it any longer." Her sobs were not hurting me. Her betrayal had gone beyond any I have ever heard of or wrote of.

"Don't worry Edith....It's okay, you don't have to live with that knowledge any longer." I told her with a smile.

"Really?" She was surprised and was turning around just in time to see me for one last time.

I took the trophy and slammed it against her skull, the crack of the bone made me sure that she was dead. Blood ran down poor Edith's face. I took her outside to the swimming pool where I dropped her in slowly and with a splash the cloud of red filled the pool. Down to the bottom of the pool Edith Larson went, and just like she had always wanted things to be laid to rest in my mind. There she was in her elegant age, laid to rest at the bottom of the pool on Mitron Street.

* * * * *

As I walked up to the main entry way of the Sir Francis Drake hotel, I could feel the anxiety in my body rising. Lily made me nervous. This was the first time she had taken over one of my books because before then it was Pricter's job. I wondered what she was going to say when I into the lobby, I gripped tightly to my briefcase and walked inside.

When I entered the lobby, Lily was sitting at the table with a man I recognized and a man that I didn't know or so I thought.

"Hi, Ed! I'm so glad that you could join us." Oh yes, how glad you are to lure me to this place with my old friend and someone who I hadn't seen for ten years, I thought to myself. The man sitting next to Peter was Officer Jimmy Nicolas although this time he was in a red and green sweater and beige slacks instead of the blood covered uniform I saw him last.

"It's a pleasure to see you again Ed." Peter said.

"Same here." said Officer Nicolas.

"Listen." Lily said noticing my nervous tension. "Mr. Nicolas is so happy that he has found you and would like to ask you a few questions and then we can get to your book." She said that such an easiness, but what Lily did not know was that last time Mr. Nicolas went questioning, he got a little to close to truth and that was when he and I were standing at the death scene of Edith.

I stood by the edge looking down at the now deteriorating Edith at the bottom of my pool. It was the next morning and I had come out to see what had become of Edith during the night; her flesh was as blue as the water when rinsed with cleaner. The chlorine must have taken its toll on Edith's face, because I could see little pieces of rotting flesh hanging from her forehead. Her fingers looked hard and twisted; the rigor mortis made her hands seem as if they were coral at the bottom of the clear ocean.

I decided that I would wait awhile before calling the authorities. I wanted them to think that I was just coming home from all the meetings and book signings that I had, so I went inside and took a shower. The water was rolling down my face when I thought how wonderful it would be if I could get away with this horrid crime.

After my shower I got dressed and went outside to our car, got inside and drove over to the nearest rest stop. That is where I called the authorities.

"Solano County, this is Officer Nicolas, how can I help you? " The voice on the other end sounded very young.

"Yes, this is Edward Larson. I would like someone to go check on my wife, my address is 4277 Mitron Street," I said, sounding worried.

"What is the reason for this call, sir?" the young man on the other end said.

"I have been trying to call her, no one is answering and I would like to know if she is okay." I thought that would be a logical reason.

"Sir, we will do everything we can to make sure that your wife is okay." The young man seemed confident, but I was confident he wasn't going to find her "okay".

When I pulled up to the house, there was only one squad car there. There was this boy standing in my driveway. It looked as though it was Halloween and he was just another trick or treater. There was no way that this boy was the cop that found Edith, was there?

The boy took off his dark aviator sunglasses, looked down at the front of the car, and jotted something down in his little notebook.

I got out of the car and the boy came up to me, shook my hand, and said," Morning Mr. Larson, my name is Officer Jimmy Nicolas. I am afraid that I have some bad news for you, sir." I could see that this was his first time telling a person about the death of their loved one. Hell, I bet this was the first time the kid had even seen a dead body or had been out in the field even.

"Mr. Larson, it seems that your wife has had a horrible accident." He looked down and I could see that it was hard for him to come out with the right words.

"It seems as though your wife has slipped and hit her head on the side of the pool, before she fell in...Sir, your wife is dead." This was the first time that I had heard the news actually put in front of me. It was real; she was gone and I knew it was real because someone else had viewed her and confirmed that she was dead.

"Oh, no, not Edith. Not my love-how could this have happened? She was always so careful." Tears ran down my face, but to which Officer Nicolas was witnessing the tears that I cried were not the tears of sadness nor were they tears of hurt, No, these tears were the drops of freedom, for the only two people that knew the awful truth about me were dead.

"I have a few questions for you, err... can I ask you a few questions?" asked the young man.

"I'm not sure what I can do for you, but I guess you can" I wasn't really afraid of what he would ask since he didn't seem he had the procedure down right in the first place I mean, what kind of officer do you know would have to correct himself when trying to investigate a suspect? I was waiting for him to ask questions about the last time Edith and I had spoken or last seen each other, how our relationship was, and if we had any problems but I will tell you what; what he said next surprised me.

"We have witnesses that saw your car leaving the home of Colin Louvaille last week around the time he was found dead."

Here my wife lies dead on the bottom of our pool and this deputy asks me about being at Colin's house?

"I wasn't there I have been out of town. I have been at meetings and signings the last two days I had no time to go visit Colin."

"Mr. Larson, Mr. Louvaille died last week, not in the last two days. I need you to get your story straight."

* * * * *

I sat down at the table next to Lily, Peter, and Officer Nicolas. I could tell by the gray hair on his head that he must have been through a lot since Edith's death. I could tell that he had something that he wanted to tell me. I really hoped he wasn't going to interrogate me. I wasn't up to Nicolas' sly questions. I was tired; I knew the end was near for me both in literature life and in life in general. I was worn out in my older age-and cold. The lobby was freezing.

I could see that Officer Nicolas was looking straight at me. Even though his eyes wanted to meet, mine did not.

"Mr. Larson, you didn't ever tell me your story of what you were doing the night that Colin Louvaille was murdered." His words were a haunting sound.

"I did too! You just don't remember because you were too busy wondering what happened to Colin more you were about my wife." I met eyes with him this time.

"You do not understand, I indeed was worried about the cause of your wife's death...." I could tell by the way he paused he was going to have something to add.

"Oh you were! Were you? Then why do you keep bringing me up in Colin's death too then and now? I was afraid of where he was going with the whole thing; I think I was more afraid of not being able to shut up before he would be able to read me like a open book.

"I have reason to believe that Mrs. Larson and Mr. Louvaille' murders were linked." I knew by what he just said he was onto a path I didn't want him to travel.

"Who said my wife's death was caused by murder?." I asked hoping that he would agree that I was right and than leave me and the subject alone.

"Who said it wasn't Mr. Larson? Who said that your wife and Mr. Louvaille's lives weren't taken by the same person?" With that statement I knew I had to do something to make him quit...but what I did not know...but wait....maybe?"

* * * * *

The night was just another usual night for a summer, the air was hot and the stars shone bright for there were no clouds in the sky to dim their illumination. As I walked up the front pathway to 2118 Mitron Drive I gazed upon the nameplate above the door which read " *Come and tell your tale at the home of Colin Louvaille.*" That was Colin for you Everything had to do with writing...every aspect of this man's life had to do with writing.

I opened the door to Colin's house and started to walk in I knew that it being nine-thirty Colin had probably retired for the night and spent the rest of his evening upstairs. Colin's house was a grand Victorian style house which had two couches facing each other. One on either side of a glass coffee table with golden legs. In the corner of the room was a grand cherry walnut desk that had upon it all the manuscripts of all the authors that were published through M.P.P.

I wanted to get near that desk, therefore taking the copy of my latest book that Edith and I wrote and destroying it. It was called **Behind Him,** The book was written about Pat Nixon and her non-fiction relationship she had with Richard; how she comes to tell how all the good that was done while he was in office was her idea and how she was going to tell of the Watergate Scandal and the deep destruction it would have done if she would have told before the scandal took place.

I went over to the desk to pick up the manuscript; it was lying on the top of the stack because I had just given it to Colin not even five hours earlier. It was then that I heard a noise from coming from up stairs, "Oh Mr. Louvaille, this is great!" I must have came at the wrong time it seemed as though Louvaille was up to one of his personal female client affairs. Colin had the tendency to shun the female race when it came to their writings and their talents. "He didn't want to see the writings until he saw their talents in bed" as he would say.

I turned to leave but the utter existence of curiosity that came over me made me stay, I shouldn't have stayed. If I were to know what it would cost me or Colin, I wouldn't have stayed at all. Sometimes things are better left alone and not to be heard or seen. Sometimes the desire of needing to know something can cost a person way more than how the feeling and want of knowing is. What I heard was not just an ordinary female voice, uh uh. What I heard was the voice of my dear and beloved Edith!

I ducked behind the sofa, waiting for what seemed like days, and then there it was; Edith and Colin appeared in front of me. Colin had a robe on and Edith was leaning over and thanking him for what he had done for her that night. *That rotten scoundrel! He took advantage of my Edith.* I had a feeling that what she wanted was love and some understanding but if she needed it she could have came to me. I waited for Edith to leave and that is when I was outraged with the extreme hatred that is only felt by a person who has a friend who betrays them. A friend who takes a person's very life and meddles where they don't belong! No one can do such a thing to Edward Larson and get away with it! Not a friend, not a loved one, NO ONE.

* * * * *

"I have nothing else to tell you, Mr. Nicolas, about that night other than I was staying the night at a hotel that was on the way back to town." I didn't want to be at the table with him anymore. I was trying to put it all behind me and yet another thing reminded me of Edith. I knew she was mad even in her death. I didn't know how much of **Behind Him** was just like what I had done to Edith, but she was not letting me forget my betrayal, just as no one betrays Edward Larson it is the same with Edith Larson.

I started to get up from the table and head for the door, wrapping my scarf tightly around my neck, wondering if I should just end it there before anyone knew of what I was hiding, They didn't need to know the real Edward Larson; they needed to know that I was great and always would be.

"Well then Mr. Larson, if you think of anything else you could have been doing that night, you give me a call," Officer Nicolas said while he handed me a card that read: *Officer James T. Nicolas, Sheriff, 555-8790*. I almost wanted to laugh at the thought of that Barney Fife ten years ago made it to be Sheriff today.

"Well, Ed, are you going to show me the half—finished manuscript yet?" I shook my head.

"I will let you see it tomorrow when we don't have so much company and we can actually talk about it." I smiled a half a smile, using it to point at Peter.

"What's the matter? Are you afraid that an old friend might steal your ideas!?" He laughed but I did not find him to be humorous.

"No, that is not what I was implying...." I prolonged the "implying," which probably gave it away.

"Are you telling the truth, Ed?" he laughed once again and still not dawning a smirk from the likes of I.

* * * * *

I followed Colin to the room at the back of the house that was the bathroom. I couldn't wait anymore. When he took off his robe I thought of that dirty old man's body on my wife. I needed to teach him a lesson; a sort of teaching that Colin wouldn't ever forget and neither would I.

"Colin!" I could tell that he was frightened as he turned around with eyes widened so much he could have fit the Grand Canyon in them.

"EDWARD!!" he screamed, while he grabbed his robe to cover his worthless, womanizing body.

"Colin...don't look so scared...I just thought I would drop by to say hi." I could see the wretched old man was nervous it was like an ocean in the room with all the sweat that he was pouring out.

"Uhh....hi...Uhh...can you go now, Ed...I have to take a shower....uh...BIG DAY tomorrow! 'Behind Him' goes to print!" I could smell his fear and I could feel his skin tremble. Being a writer I guess you make a little thing like a freaked out employer to be something you would read in a horror book.

"Why, Colin? So you can wash away your guilt about sleeping with my wife!!" I couldn't keep the nice guy act anymore.

"Edward, trust me...I didn't touch Edith...I tell you the truth...She came to me with an idea and being your wife I took it...." I didn't believe a word that he said. I just didn't trust him. I knew what I knew and I hated to be told otherwise. He should know that more than anyone; he and I worked together for years.

"I DON'T trust you." My hands started to clench his neck.

"I tell you the truth, Edward!!!!" he yelled in my face.

"The TRUTH is in the eye of the beholder and what I beheld is you're a lying, backstabbing...son of a bitch!"

I took the rope that tied Colin's robe and forced it around his neck, pulling tight with every shrug he let out.

"Edward, you will pay for this....you will fail...ehh....You will be a light to writers no more...uhh." And with that Colin was dead.

I couldn't believe what I had just done, or could I? This was the first person that I had ever killed!" Did I really just kill another human being in cold blood?" I was questioning myself and what I had become. It was as if I were a animal hungered for too long and then let loose to finally eat.

I was just leaving the Sir Francis Drake hotel when I heard from above me a loud crack and snapping of cords. I looked up just in time to notice one of the glass elevators coming down toward me.

"Watch out!" I heard screams and gasps from all around me I jumped out of the way just in time to see the mammoth of glass and metal falling toward the ground my footing hit the curb, sending me to the ground and just missing me like some action hero just narrowly escaping an inevitable death. I watched in horror as I saw in the reflection of the glass right before it hit the ground. A reflection of death yet again; the reflection of Edith.

Why? Why was it that she was haunting me now? What had I done to deserve this? I had come to peace with myself I thought, but by the looks of it Edith had not come to peace with her own immortality. She needed to feed on my mind. The very thought of making me go insane inside perhaps turned her on in a way which was dark and demonic, almost enough to send vile into my mouth.

The day was dark, the sky intoxicated by gray wool moving slowly in the wind. The rain fell hard against the window pane and the wind blew so hard that I thought at any moment the windows of the cabin were going to break. The only sound coming from in the house was the ever so quiet whispering from two people who knew so little, but at the same time knew too much.

"Edward" I heard from behind me as I put my sunglasses on. I had known that the day would let out no sunlight, but the fear that someone would see the gleam of success in my eyes dawned on me which brought on the odd apparel. It was John. He walked over behind me and pressed his hands down on my shoulders. He spoke as he softly shook me at the same time. "I am sorry that you had to lose two friends so close together...Edith was like a sibling to me."

I got angered a bit by his comment. A sibling she was not to him. I knew for a long time that they were close somehow; a connection that I did not know, but was going to find out later.

I was walking toward the door getting ready to go outside to the car when I heard Edith's parents talking rather loudly from upstairs.

"You think Edward did it?" her father said to his wife.

I started up the staircase to the bedroom where Edith's parents were nosing around I had told them they could get any belongings of Edith's that they thought that they wanted and what they deserved but what they did not deserve was to talk about me at a time like this and what business did they have if any to question the death of their daughter to me?.

Mr. Merrill was five foot four with a balding head speckled with liver spots his hair looked like a pearl white toilet bowl wrapped almost three hundred and sixty degrees around his head. He had a mustache that rested over his top lip, slowly creeping into his mouth.

Mrs. Merrill was six foot, a very slender woman. She had dark gray hair all tightened up in what looked like monkey bread. Both she and Mr. Merrill's profiles looked like they were melting where they stood as both of them were very old and their health was deteriorating.

These two reminded me of John Steinbeck's book **Of Mice and Men;** Mrs. Merrill being Lenny and Mr. Merrill being George.

Mrs. Merrill was as sweet as her daughter was before she betrayed me. Her smile would send you into a tranquil relaxing state. Mr. Merrill, on the other hand, was into conservatism. He liked everything the same way as it was about fifty years ago.

"I think she should have made him go to work...real work like steel processing not to cloud his mind with silly fantasies." I almost wanted to spill my secret there and tell them that is was their daughter who "filled her mind with silly fantasies."

"Oh, Dale, don't say that again! You had dreams too once" she told him, a little angered.

"Yes, I know Patricia, but that was all they stayed dreams. People dream of being ball players, musicians, actors, but only to realize that they are stuck in being just what they are. Regular men; regular people," he answered her back.

"I think you need to go lay down, Dale your blood pressure will be very high if you stay in this kind of mood, dear." Patricia motioned him to lie down on the bed.

I walked back down the stairs before they noticed me.

"Edward!" I heard Patricia call from in the bedroom. "Could you bring me Dale's pills? They are in the tote bag next to the front door."

I walked slowly to the front door-very slowly, almost in slow motion, hoping that maybe the old man would croak before I could bring him his colorful array of tic tacs.

How could he think it was me? I questioned my conscience. *Did he know that I had done it? What was he going to say?!!!.* "Oh, Dale to think that you can get me to succumb to my wrong doings and appease yourself? You're wrong Dale Merrill, just as your daughter was...NO ONE gets in the way of Edward D. Larson!"

When I opened the pill box, a piece of paper was taped to it, a note that read: **Do Not Mix Excedrin with Blood Pressure Meds.**

"Edward!" John called from the other room. "I only have room for the folding chairs you're going to have to take Dale and Patricia to Mon'ame."

"Alright." I said. This was the perfect time to play out my sly plan and so I was to kill Dale, and maybe even Patricia, oh so carefully.

We head toward Mon'ame Cemetery, about seventy miles north of Emerald Lake.

I coaxed Mrs. Merrill and the already drowsy Mr. Merrill to my black nineteen forty-eight De Soto. They opened their doors and got in. This was going to be the last ride that one of them, or perhaps both of them, would ever take. I hadn't figured out the full extent of my plan yet.

"I don't want to go! I can't believe she's dead, Patricia; our little girl. Our baby!" I heard Mr. Merrill cry from the back seat.

"Calm down, Dale. Edith is alright now. She is in heaven. She's waiting for us." Mrs. Merrill said, trying to calm her hyperventilating husband.

"Oh you don't have to wait any longer!" I said, pulling a pistol from the glove compartment and shooting both Dale and Edith point blank in the head.

"Edward, can you give Dale his blood pressure medicine?" Patricia's voice woke me from my daydreaming state I looked back to realize that they were both still alive and breathing, I look in the glove compartment to find it practically empty with just a few napkins and a road map. I knew that was all too easy and would point the finger to me indefinitely.

"Of course!" I reached into the box and grabbed the big white horse pill and gave it to Mrs. Merrill in which she shoved down the old man's throat.

I was watching the shadow of the trees hitting the hood of the already darkened De Soto I could imagine these dark figures that were being cast on the hood as a dark masquerade of demons eating away at a dark soul a dark soul called my own heart.

As the minutes passed they felt like hours I glanced back to see both Mr. and Mrs. Merrill asleep, I saw my chance and I took it I changed the clock on Mrs. Merrill' watch to read three o' clock even though it was still one thirty.

"Patricia.." I said trying to wake her up. "Patricia, isn't it time for Dale to take his other pill?"

"Huh?" she said looking down at her wristwatch. "Oh yes! Is it three o' clock already?" she seemed a little confused.

"Yes it is," I replied as I handed her the Excedrin, thinking how keen and smart I was to put the life of Edith's father into the hands of Edith's mother. I had to bite down hard on my tongue to stop myself from smiling.

She handed him the pill in which he swallowed down his old floppy throat with his hidden elixir in which he kept in the flask at his side.

I could imagine this mystery elixir for sure alcoholic mixing the medicines together slowly and silently. Dale had not knowingly just mixed up his poison and only time would now kill the wretched old man.

Mrs. Merrill went back to sleep and I slowly changed her wristwatch back to one thirty three. I watched as I drove by many lakes to get to Mon'ame the cold November had froze the tops of them just slightly making them look as if they were the tops of glass tables.

"Wow." I thought to myself, "Look at the glass...Look at the glass..."

* * * * *

"Look at all that glass. That man was fo' sho a goner!"

I looked around me and I could see the remnants of glass, the way the sun beams hit them while they fell looked like fireflies flying in light snowfall ever now and then you could see a piece of glass shine just as it was about to hit the cold hard pavement. I was shaken and startled about what had just happened to me or more-less about what could have happened to me. The chapters of my horror were slowly unfolding and here she was; Edith sill in her own glory, reigning over my life, turning each page with me caught in the midst.

I couldn't let myself stay there. I needed to find somewhere to hide. The public could not see me like this; not Edward Larson. How would I feel if my profile dawned the next mornings National Enquirer magazine: **Edward Larson Old and Alone, tries to commit suicide on the streets of San Francisco.** I wouldn't know what to think about my own self. My reputation was on the line and I did not want anyone who knew me or knew of me to find me on my ass in the middle of the street. So I got up quick and hobbled to the nearest alleyway to get out of the sight of any reporters.

It was an old and cold alleyway, dark and weather beaten like myself; I seen a rusting piece of sheet metal and some old towels with the initials SFD; probably some old inventory from within the hotel, I carefully picked up the sheet metal and placed it against a big blue dumpster sitting on the far end of the alleyway near a brick wall. I climbed behind it, covered myself with the giant towels and went to sleep.

"Oh, I know what others don't know with a rinka dink dink and a dung dee doe." I heard this odd voice singing from inside the trash can.

I had almost forgotten where I was but was awoken by the singing of this out of tune siren, plus the raining of garbage on my head. I sat there quietly, still listening to what this person or creature was saying, not wanting them to know my presence but the curiosity lingered in my mind of what this person might have held in their mind.

"I know he killed her, I know he killed them. I know the truth and so does he," the voice went on.

My head began to sweat and my blood began to boil. Fear spread across me like a wildfire ignited by this person's words. How did they know? They weren't talking about me!? Surely not! This has to be a dream. I told myself but realized quickly it wasn't. I heard the sound of someone grunting and heard something hard slide down the sheet metal, only a thin piece of heavy metal separated I and this person who knew too much and then it happened this person moved the metal.

"You're in my spot!" There in front of me stood a woman crouched over as if her back were a stone bridge that was bent and could not move. Her teeth were stained with dried blood that looked like black pus; this puss would shower as she talked.

"Did you hear me, sir? Are you deaf? YOU'RE IN MY SPOT!" She came a little closer this time and in the light so I could see her better. Her body smelled also like Harold's breath and old horse urine. Her hair was dark and matted, with tiny white specks, which looked like maggots nesting in her oil compounded hairs. Some looked forever trapped in her twisted mane.

"You don't hear very good do you, Mr. Larson?" I was shocked that she knew who I was but could not speak for the way she looked at me made me cold; her eyes sending me into a trance. They were as cold as a blue sapphire in the icy Atlantic.

I tried once again to get a word out but couldn't. I did not know whether it was from fright or from being afraid of puking when I opened my mouth. This hideous woman made me sick not only by her looks and her eye slicing smell but because of her song of what she had said and of how she knew me so well to address me as Mr. Larson.

"What's the matter, Ed? Someone knows your secret? Oh, don't be surprised...You knew it was going to come along sooner or later," She said as she pointed her bony finger at me which the bone I could see through her skin. Her nails were long, jagged, stuffed underneath each nail looked as what might be bone marrow.

She did know too much, I was just about to grab her by the neck when she darted off toward the lit end of the alley, going into the city streets. I composed myself and went after her, but the sun blinded my view since my pupils weren't use to the bright light yet and when my eyes finally adjusted, she had already vaporized it seemed in the glaze of the morning sun.

"Who was that? I was so confused, so scared, and so sick I could hardly walk as I stumbled down the cracked sidewalk I looked down at the stains on the cement from other people's feet, knowing that she that knew my secret. She who bound me to an unstoppable thought probably lurked down this same stretch. sidewalk; I pulled my P-coat tight together, trying to block the cold wind of the past and the present from my body.

When we finally reached Mon'ame Cemetery, the wait of death was still in the progress there in the black De Soto. I was just hoping and waiting for the old man to take his last breath of oxygen, waiting for him to gasp with agony, but it seemed that the Grim Reaper was taking an intermission at this time-perhaps he went out for a smoke?

"Oh, what a dreary day it is," exclaimed Mrs. Merrill from the back.

"What do you want it to be, Patricia? Bright and sunny, cheerful and over joyously abundant with birds singing?" Floppy Throat nagged.

Oh I wish that pill would just hurry up and kick in. What was taking it so long? Please free me from this bastard! He needs to die! Waiting! Come on! Take it! Let me watch as you tremble with fear! Let me see your anguish, your terror! Why isn't it happening? I couldn't deal with this anger any longer right before we got to the cemetery I saw one chance that could maybe kill us all but at least would kill him.

I saw one last glass topped lake; Mon'ame Lake, the lake that sat next to the cemetery. I knew with the roads already laced with black ice this could look for sure like an accident, I pressed on the gas pedal hoping to slide into the icy water of the lake. Oh, how I hated to lose my car but this was more important. I needed to rid of Floppy Throat. I needed to silence the man who knew too much and so it went-there we were sliding sideways toward the lake.

"EDWARD, WHAT'S GOING ON!?" I heard Patricia scream from the back. I hated to put her in the middle of this but I couldn't just throw her out of the car.

"YOU'RE GOING TO KILL US, IDIOT!" Floppy Throat was all the way awake now just in time to see his death.

As we hit the lake, the sound of thunder clapped in the air the sound of breaking ice surrounded us and giant arms of sub zero water came in through the windows to grasp the heavy De Soto and pull it to the bottom of the lake. I looked back just in time to see the water hit Dale in the face. He stared at me while it happened, his eyes looking at me but his sight I could tell was already gone, I could not see what had happened to Patricia but wasn't able to see much for that is when I watched as the sky became blurred and my eyes were stabbed with ice as the car was now completely submerged.

The temperature of the water stung me all over I could not stand one more minute of being in the water. Somehow I made it out the window even though the force of the De Soto was pulling me down with it was it; like a tug of war with a metal giant.

. My motor skills were being diluted by the frigid volume of water that I had put myself in. I started to swim to the top of the water, trying to use every amount of strength I had to make it to the top. I could only remember someone yelling my name and darkness total darkness compressed my body and it was lights out for the time being for me.

* * * * *

I whistled for a taxi. I need to get away from the inland of San Fran and toward the water.

"Taxi!" I waved my hand, hoping that a yellow hearse would come my way.

I stepped off the curb a little to get into the dirty old cab and nearly tripped. I did not know whether it was my own clumsiness or just the drainage of strength that the Bloodsprayer had taken from me. I slowly got into the cab and settled myself in the tar stained back seat, looking up at the driver. I was just waiting for a Hindu or Arabian. You know, your stereotypical taxi driver, but instead it was a man; not too much younger than I.

"Where can I take you, sir?" The man asked, glancing over his frameless eyeglasses and looking in the rearview mirror.

"Take me to..." My mind shuffled through all the places that I had already been and all the people that I had seen.

"Sir, I don't mean to be rude, but the meter is running," the man said, pointing at his dash.

"Just give me a second, okay? I will pay you for the entire time I am using up." If I just strangled him, I could go wherever the Hell I wanted.

My mind was a total mess at the time. *Should I kill him? Where Should I go? Can I just run away out of the line sight of everyone?* My thoughts dwindled in my mind but were abruptly snuffed when I thought of what the Bloodsprayer had said, "You don't hear very good do you, Mr. Larson?"

"Take me to—" And then it hit me. The Bloodsprayer was not the first to call me by name. If I could have only asked him then how he knew who I was, would things be different?

"Take me to Captain's Corner!," I said hoping that Harold would be able to let me into his mind I found a door and was about ready to open it.

"That's quite a way, mister! Are you sure you want to go there?" The man looked at me, confused.

"Yes, yes indeed I want to go there!" I was ready to open Pandora's Box, it seemed to me.

I would have thought nothing of it if Harold would have called me Ed or Mr. Larson, for the stature that I had and The LEGEND that went along with it, but the case was not that at all. Harold called me 'Larson the Arson' and the only people that knew about that name was people that knew me for years, I did not let that story go far; didn't want anyone to think badly of me, you know?

While we drove along the crowded streets back to Captain's Corner, I couldn't help but wonder what it was that Harold had locked away in his mind that I wanted so badly to hold the key to and unlock a way to find out the truth on how he knew me and where he heard that story from that gave me the name Larson the Arson.

I had the window down, feeling the cool brisk air, wondering why it was that Edith wanted to haunt me now. *Was it my imagination or was it really happening? Was the woman who once helped me coming back for revenge and the apology that she deserved?*

"Sir, is there something wrong with you? You seem a little pale," the taxi driver asked me.

"No, I am fine, thank you. I don't need you nosing around in my business!" I snapped back at him.

We stopped at a stop light and while we sat there in the cold, yet dead heat of air, I believed brought on by my fear and anger, I looked up, glancing up at one of the windows. I do not know what made me look up there, but my wandering eyes caught a glimpse of something that made the blood clot in the vessels of my eyes. It was if the anger that I had was cooking the blood just by what I saw. High above the city street on the roof of an old building, there she stood, perched and staring straight at me. Not Edith, but Bloodsprayer.

"Stop! I need to go no further, you hear me?" I got out of the cab in all fuss and rush of adrenaline and headed out the door that bound me to the yellow hearse and darted toward the building, shouting out to the woman above me. I shouted "I will

get you and throw you off that roof you hear me!!?" I raised my hand a stuck up my middle finger.

Oh, the anger inside. The burning desire to watch that woman fall to her death, not to utter another word of what she knew or what she had seen...if she knew or seen anything. I was just about to doubt the fact that this woman knew anything, until I heard her words ringing through the air.

I do not know if my mind was completely shut off to the outside world by this point or the anger shuttered reality from actuality but I could have sworn that I did not see a single soul around me; just me and Bloodsprayer. Having my eyes shot right at her above me. I knew I should have walked away but her song her wretched song. "Shut the hell up!"

"Oh, I know what others don't know with a rink a dink dink and a dung dee doe," she sang down to me like an angel of Hell in demonic exaltation.

"You said I was the one who was deaf! You are the one whose ears are probably filled with wax so thick it stands erect out of each earlobe."

"I know you killed her, I know you killed them. I know the truth and so do you." There she was pointing that bony finger.

"Who!? Who did I kill?" I wanted to know what she knew... *Ahh! What the hell did she know?* I thought to myself.

"Come up here, Edward, and I will tell you." She motioned her finger to a door below.

As I slammed through the door, I climbed each step faster than the next. I would get up there and throw the old bitch from the roof before any Friscan heard her.

My hair fell in front of my face, the gray hair swayed in my eyesight. I could tell how old I was getting and that bothered me and it also bothered me that I lived with these secrets for this long before telling anyone and I still didn't have it in my soul to tell anyone and didn't want Bloodsprayer to do the honors.

I got to the cold frigid metal door that separated me once again from this woman whose acapella I wanted so strongly to mute.

I got the courage to turn the knob; my conscience was getting to me. *Do not kill another soul, Edward Larson; you will be damned to the sizzling infernos of Hell.* I knew that I could not throw this woman from aloft, even if I pleased, too many people down below would view my notorious crime.

As I passed the passageway to Bloodsprayer's Lair, the momentum of time stopped in its place. I spun around everywhere looking for Bloodsprayer.

"Where'd you go!?" This couldn't have been my mind playing tricks on me. No, this was real I saw her...I *heard* her.

No one.

Even though I was not dead, I already felt like I was in the pits of Hell. The agony that dawned over my body was not to be shaken off. Here I was, Edward Larson, defeated, old, and beaten. My legs felt as if they were shackled to the ground....my ankles were crushed in blistering pain and my mind in oblivion, straining for yet another answer.

I walked to the edge of the building, in the state of mind that I would do it, end it all there. I would stand on the ledge and shoot myself in the head falling eight stories to the man made pathway below. I could already imagine it there I would be lying in the cold blood that I brewed over the years, bathing in crimson, the demons liquid oozing from my body and steady trickle of blood running from the side of my mouth and onto the earth's floor. My eyes filled with tears just think how beautiful it would feel to see me Author of Mystery on the front page of the paper; drowning, if not dead already, in my own blood.

When I awoke, I was lying in a cabin on a cot in the middle of a room. I was greeted by the man who helped Edith and I build the lake house. A short long haired hippie with the lengthy beard and beads hanging from his neck. Al Rigit, the man who I owed my very life too, was Al Rigit; Stoner of the Year.

"You know you shouldn't go swimming in waters you can't wade in," Al said with a eerie chuckle.

The smell of soup filled the air. I looked at myself lying there. I looked under the covers, only to find myself completely naked.

"The folks at Emerald Lake told us that you should stay here awhile, didn't they, Mr. Sivle?"

Al was talking to his pet Owl. The old thing looked near death. It was almost uncanny to a dusty old knick knack. I didn't know why he kept that whooping thing but then again I had no room to talk down or think badly of this man. He did save my life.

"What happened, Albert?" That was the first time I thought I was crazy and it definitely was not the last.

"You crashed into one of the lakes here in Mon'ame next to the cemetery," he started.

"I did?" I pretended like I was shocked by this news of such calamity.

"Dale and Patricia, were they hurt?" I was so intrigued by the fact that by some possibility he would let me know at least Floppy Throat was.

"Who?" He was confused, I could tell.
"Edith's parents, were they hurt in the crash? Did they drown? Details Al...I WANT DETAILS." I was getting quite flustered at this point.

"Ed, calm down!" I could tell he was very distraught by confusion and I bet he was down right scared.
"Ed..." he continued. "You were the only one in the vehicle when it fell into the lake."

How could this be? I thought to myself. They were there. I'd seen them, didn't I? For sure this has been some kind of mistake, I saw Old Floppy Throat staring at me.

"But I drove them to the cemetery," This I for sure wanted explanations for.

"Yes, I know but when you left the cemetery you said you wanted to be alone." Al held his hand to my forehead, possibly searching for a temp.

"The cemetery? I never made it to the cemetery."

"Yes, you did, I was there, remember?"

Slowly, I went to thinking. Yes...the Old Hip was right, I had made it to the cemetery, I got mad because they had already put Edith into the ground. I was pissed.

"Yeah, Patricia and Dale said you kept ranting on about some kind of mixture."

"They were talking about a mixture?" Clammy hands, nausea, and anger started to fill my body. *How much did Al Rigit know?*

"Yeah, but that doesn't matter right now, does it, Mr. Sivle? I want you to rest and not worry about anything. That was months ago."
"Months?"

"You've been asleep since fall. It's spring now. You were in a state basically identical to a coma. The only thing keeping you alive was that," He pointed at my arm.

I looked down at my arm noticing a long tube running from a long metal coat hanger-looking object with a bag full of green bean looking liquid. It was an IV

"So what happened to Edith's parents?"

"Well, Mr. and Mrs. Merrill stayed with John since Mr. Merrill was in really bad shape, complaining of stomach problems." He shook his head from side to side.

"How is he?" I asked, wondering if I had ended Floppy Throat's life.

"Ed, Dale Merrill is dead. He died of a spurt of massive blood flow to the brain, but none of that matters right now. Everyone knows it was an accident."

"An accident? What do you mean?" What was an accident? His death or the fact that I fell into an icy cold lake?"

He hesitated and opened his mouth for a second, only to close it seconds later.

"Al, I want to know, tell me what was an accident?" His muteness was taunting my mind.

"If I tell you—" he blurted out one second and denied what he had just said.

"No, Rigit! You started, now tell me! I have a right to know what you are talking about." My blackened heart had no room for a lingering thought.

"You have to promise to rest, Ed, and leave the worrying up to me." He cleared his throat.

"Go on." My mind was speaking to me yet again. *Waiting Rigit, your time will be close to an end if you don't hurry up. You're making me mad, hero or not.*

Al stroked his beard a few times and fiddled with his fingers continuously. I was about ready to chop his digits off but remembered I was naked; lucky him.

"We believe...They believe that through all the confusion of the death and the anger, you were feeling against people accusing you for the death of your wife you-."

"I DID WHAT? Oh, no, not again. You're going to blame me for the death of Dad, too!?" I needed to look innocent as pure as freshly fallen snow.

"Ed, you did give Mrs. Merrill the medications at the wrong time, the autopsy reports show that, not that you did it necessarily.

"So you think that I killed him!?" I was about ready to rip out the IV out of my arm and jab it into the neck of the flippin' hippie.

"You didn't do it on purpose, Ed. Times just got messed up, that was all. No one or nothing says it was deliberate.

"No one, yeah right. I know how those people think they do not think like you or I. Well maybe just I. They need drama in their lives 'cause they're lowlifes."

I could tell by Al's face that he was getting nervous. He looked as if he were a little boy standing in line for a roller coaster that scared him straight out of his wits or perhaps even a performer waiting for their turn on stage. I was too weak to even try to attempt another murder. I watched Al change the green frog spit in the mistletoe of a pouch above my head and slowly but surely I was off to sleep.

I opened my eyes to find myself once again in Al Rigit's cabin but things were different this time. Things were so much different; not only did I find myself clothed, but I found myself sitting upright. Scattered on the couch was carnage of indescribable pieces. That's right; pieces...not of a human being. No couldn't have been a human being, much too small and unless this person was an Indian or some kind of angel, the feathers didn't account for much.

I looked around for any kind of forced entry, but found none. I knew that Al was gone for his VW was not in the driveway. The smell was strong enough to burn your nose hairs and bring chunks of food up your throat. The soothing smell of chicken soup loomed in the oxygen no longer but the sour smell of burnt hair or some kind of hair-like follicle.

Who left the stove on? I went over to turn the knob and glanced down at the sight before me in the sauce pan. I then understood what the smell was and where the concoction of meat and feathers came from. There in the pan I saw it; a sight that made me feel like I wanted to gouge my own eyes out and slam them to the ground. Next to the stove I found the mistletoe pouch, when I looked down and found that the tube was no longer embedded in my forearm but now ran into the mouth of a bodiless cooked head of Mr. Sivle.

What was I going to say to Rigit when he got home to find his feathered friend a pile of mulch on the couch? What would he do? On second thought, what would I do? I started cleaning up, hoping that there would be some way I could quarantine the place before Al returned, but the stench that surrounded me the heavy cloud of death made me know that there was no way of denying that something gruesome and "fowl" went on in the cabin.

By the time I was nearly exhausted, the head and remains of Mr. Sivle plus a few blood stained towels and washcloths were buried in Rigit's backyard. I sprinkled some baking soda on the spot where Mr. Sivle's chunks had dwelled and flipped the cushion over, hoping to hide the stain that would have me questioned on the spot...literally.

I found it hard to jab the IV into my forearm again but the pain wasn't as bad as the pain I would feel having to explain the death of Mr. Sivle to Al Rigit. Even if I wanted to, I could not say what or how it happened. I stripped down to nothing yet again to lie cold and naked under the sheet that lay on the cot.

I heard Rigit's van outside. I closed my eyes and opened them again, hoping that the last few hours were a dream but the perch was still empty where Mr. Sivle use to sit and the stench was lingering in the air. The stench? *Oh, Hell, I forgot about the stench!*

I heard the key in the doorknob and then the deadlock...It was time to face reality.

The thoughts of suicide subsided just as fast as they had showed up in my mind. I stepped away from the ledge of the building.

"Where am I?" I asked myself coming back to reality and then I remembered I was on top of a building in the middle, or maybe the outskirts of San Francisco and looking down I saw the yellow hearse missing.

The sun started to drip out of the sky above me and into a horizon in the distance and it was getting cold. I knew that the temperature had fallen but what could it be that made my insides feel so cold? I felt as if I had frozen lungs in my body, my veins had the feeling of ice water running through them, murderous ice water crawling up to my head, in my mind I envisioned my own eyes blood vessels turning a dark blue.

I grabbed my handkerchief to wipe the frost from my brow. That is when I stopped to listen to the sounds in my head, the sounds that didn't make any sense but what did anymore?

"Stop, Edith!" I heard my own voice scream within me.

"No, Edward Larson, it is time!"

"What are you doing with that? Put it down! Come on, Edith, this isn't funny—PUT IT DOWN!"

I got really shaky what was I hearing, what was being broadcast through my memory. Was it my memory or was it something that I made up? A writer's mind can be his best friend and at the same time be his or her worst enemy.

I couldn't stand it anymore, looking down from the roof top. *What am I doing up here? Oh...yes; but where is she?*

Where is who? Who was I am I looking for? Am I on the hunt down for the Bloodsprayer, or was it Edith?

The connection between the Bloodsprayer and Edith, can it be one and the same? No, it couldn't be Edith is dead....isn't she? I mean, I don't actually remember seeing her after they took her body from the pool. At the funeral I don't remember being there, but at Rigit's cabin he told me that when I hit the lake Edith's parents were not in the car with me...but I saw them...didn't I? How come nobody asked me if I was all right after the elevator fell to the ground? Did it fall? The man on the Bart; my face was on the back of the book, why didn't he recognize me? Ed Larson you've gone mad!

I needed to know the answers. Who would know? Who could tell me? I ran down the rickety stairs to the sidewalk where I had envisioned my death and started to search for a pay phone.I finally found one a little ways down the block and when I got to it I skimmed hesitantly through the pages; Quincy...Quishenbery...Ralston...Riffington...RIGIT! See also Psychiatric I turned to an ad that read: Dr. Albert Rigit, If your mind's in a figit, seek Rigit. Serving San Francisco for 10 years. 555-2461.

I was just about to call the man whose bird I killed, I think? I picked up the receiver and placed it against my ear, waiting for a dial tone. The last time I had been on a pay phone was when I called the Solano County Police to tell them to check on Edith.

When the dial tone came and was a prolonged beeping in my head, I put a quarter into the phone. "Please deposit fifty cents for the next five minutes." I added another quarter.

The other end started to ring

"Hello, Dr.Rigit's office. This is Karen. Can I help you?" The woman sounded very friendly.

"Yes, is Dr. Rigit in?"

"Yes, he is. Do you need to talk to him?"

"May I ask whose calling?"

I was getting very tired of this woman's questions.

"Yes, tell him it's Edward Larson."

"Are you calling in for Mr. Larson? Does he need to change his appointment?"

"No! Just tell him that Edward Larson needs to speak with him."

"Okay, just a second ma'am."

"Ma'am?" I questioned, but Karen must have darted away because it was very silent from the other end.

I waited for probably fifteen minutes listening to some weird relaxation music when finally the familiar voice was heard again. It was Karen.

"Um, I'm really sorry, but Dr. Rigit said that he would not take the call." I knew it was probably because of the bird.

"Tell him that I am sorry about what has happened in the past. I would make it up him if I could." I really wanted to know some answers.

"I'm sorry, but I like to keep things between Dr. Rigit and I professional, and I don't need to know about his sexual affairs."

"Sexual affairs?" What was wrong with this woman? She must have been stuck with his mistletoe pouch too.

The mistletoe pouch that Al had stuck in to me was a pouch full of liquefied marijuana. He and I both know that was no ordinary medicine. Hell, he'd let Mr. Sivle lap it up.

"Did he say why?"

"Yes, he did. He said that it wasn't funny whoever you are to bring up old friends of his. especially dead ones."

I must have not comprehended right. I hope it was a misunderstanding. "Dead!?"

"Yes! Not only did Dr. Rigit turn a ghostly white, but he told me after ten years Edward Larson needs to rest in peace. No need for him to turn in his grave."

She hung up the phone before I could say anything else.

I knew something was up, but what? I needed to see Al again, but after ten years he might not want to see me. By the sounds of it he was still mad at me, but to wish death upon me, that was taking it a little too far. It was time to go see my old friend, but first I needed to go see ol' Harold. That's where I was headed when I caught a glimpse of Bloodsprayer.

I turned to look for another yellow hearse, but found none. I call them yellow hearses because you don't ever know how the driver of one is going to be and it may just as well be your last ride. I looked down the road and up, but had no luck in finding one when I remembered I was very close to my hotel. Yes that's right; I had a hotel that I was staying at. Why do you ask, didn't I stay there the night that I stayed in the alleyway? Good question. I do not know. I guess my mind was to clouded up with thoughts and visions and I was in shock.

As I walked into the hotel, I was feeling quite confident about everything and the agenda that I was about to diminish. I would ask ol' Harold how he knew me and then I was going to see Dr. Rigit and ask him for explanations of the sights and thoughts I had been thinking about. He would tell me it was stress and not to worry and I would bid him adieu and be on my way to finish my book in the peace and quiet of my hotel room, but first I need to take a nap. I was exhausted

When I got to the service counter, the lady there looked at me and probably wondered why I was so banged and battered.

"What happened to you?" She asked as she scanned my body like a MRI.

"I had a rough day," I grumbled.

"I should say. Here's your key, we were expecting you yesterday." She sounded kind of disappointed.

"Well, I'm here now! So give me the key!" I was tired and didn't feel like dealing with anyone at the time.

I looked at this woman at the counter and wondered why she worked there. *What was her life like? Did she hate it or did she love it? If she hated her life, I could just as well take it from her.* I shook the thoughts of yet another murder out of my mind. *What is wrong with you, Ed? Why are you in the mood for a killing spree? Everyone knows, Ed! EVERYONE knows! You can't hide it!*

"Your daughter left you a message. I told one of the bellhops to place it in your room." She smiled. Thinking that was going to make me feel better.

"I don't have a daughter, thank you!" *What is this, a sick joke? Someone trying to pose as a offspring of mine? Everyone knew I didn't have a child.*

"Yes, I told her that you didn't have a daughter. I've read all your books and you never mentioned her" she said nervously.
"But you took the note from her and put it in my room?" *why did she take a note from a stranger? If she knew I didn't have a daughter.*

"Yes, because she showed me two proofs of identification. She showed me a driver's license and a birth certificate."

"And what was her name?" Who was this person.

"Well the birth certificate said one name and the I.D. said another." She stumbled on her words.

"What was this person's name?" I grabbed the clerk by her collar and pulled her close up to me. She started to cry.

"I...don't remember! Eliana Larson was the name on the birth certificate!"

"And the I.D.?"

"I don't know! I can't remember! She said she was adopted and changed her name, both her first and last name." She started to turn blood red so I loosened my grip.

"Melissa! Her name was Melissa! Yeah, that's right, Melissa McKey!"

I felt as if I had swallowed my tongue. If I heard this clerk correctly, the young woman that Peter and Allison introduced Edith and I to was our own daughter. *Did Edith know this? Ahh, to Hell with everyone. Who can I trust anymore, can this be real? Who the Hell am I? Too many people to talk to and   way too little time, but I'm going to do it one way or another.*

I grabbed my room key and started up to the room. As the elevator went up to the second floor, I kept wondering about what the clerk had said. *How can this be? Edith must have known about this!* Then I remembered the time that she went to go stay with her mother. *That must have been the time she had the baby! And she left the baby why?* The elevator kept going and going, the second floor seemed so far away and then I thought about it; *I was almost struck by an elevator yesterday! What if this one falls? I won't get to read the letter!* But I closed my eyes and stayed as calm as I could. *I needed answers and if it was to risk my life on this "Hellevator" then so be it.*

I watched as the numbers lit up above the doorway and *ding.* There I was to hunt for the room that Lily had set up for me. She had come a day earlier to bring my stuff to the hotel. Room number 4A. *Where is it?* I looked up and down one side 1A, 3A and then down the other side 2A and then I feasted my eyes upon the rooms' door in its prime glory or perhaps just recently primed and then painted. Either way its glory held at least some of the answers to my questions.

I slid the key down the fancy lock on the door and walked in the room. It was dark, obviously, but it smelled like a woman's perfume. *Who was in my room?* I turned the lights on and looked around the room. Everything looked like it was part of a museum. Nothing had been touched, not a fingerprint could be found in the room, and the sheets were as stiff as a corpse. I looked on the nightstand where I told Lily to put my briefcase but instead in its place was a purse with flowery shit all over it.

"Hello?" I said as I spun around a few times.

Nothing.

"Hello! Who's in here?" I could swear I could smell a woman in my room. The smell was familiar. It was the perfume that Edith use to wear.

"Edith?" I almost had to laugh at myself for that one.

Silence.

I saw a light on through a splinter of one of the door openings. I opened it up and looked inside. What I saw in that room made my sanity dissolve yet again, face to face with the woman of death, Edith.

Edith let out a terrible scream which sent me to the ground. I was shaking and I did not want to look up.

"Are you alright?" someone asked from behind me.

It was Lily. Oh, how happy I was to see her. I was relieved, but at the same time I could not get this image of Edith out of my head. If it was like she knew that I was going to be there. *How come I didn't know that Lily was there behind me? Was she there the whole time?* I had asked her to bring my stuff to my room like my suits and my other briefcase but all that was occupying the hotel room was her stuff.

"How long have you been there?" I looked at her, I bet she could tell that I was a little frightened.

"I just walked in did I startle you?" She looked at me with wonder.

"No, I saw...never mind." If I told her she would think I was a loon, but then again she probably thought that already. There I was a full grown man settled like a baby in the middle of the floor.

"What did you see, Ed? Is someone in here?" She asked me, while she checked every nook and cranny of the room.

"No, I just need a nap. It has been a long day and I have a lot on my agenda for tomorrow."

"Well, Ed, you just rest and if you need anything just pick up your phone and call me, okay?" I knew she didn't want to leave me, but I motioned her to leave and took her advice.

I was indeed ready for a rest but I didn't dare lay in that bed without a thorough search around the room again. I probably looked like a three year old looking for the Boogey Man under my bed but I didn't want to get "Mommy" from down the hall, so I did it myself. I don't know how many times I caught myself peeking under the bed and in the bathroom before I went to bed, but I found nothing. My mind was very deep in questions upon questions, so this time I took a few muscle relaxers and went to bed.

"Edith! Please don't. I am so very sorry!"

"You should have thought about that before you killed him, you bastard!"

I knew I was dreaming first of all. My sane mind knew that Edith was dead, and second of all, I was watching all this from third person. I saw myself sitting in the study with a letter in my hand and Edith was there with her hands, choking me.

"You shouldn't have been sleeping with him!"

I couldn't believe my ears! *Who was Edith sleeping with?...Oh wait I already knew, or did I? This dream was confusing me really bad. When did this happen? It seems familiar.*

"I was doing it all for you, Edward!" She let go of my neck and backed away from me for a second.

"How could sleeping with my boss be any good for me, Edith, huh? Tell me!" Oh, yes, now I remember! I caught them sleeping together that night on Mitron Street.

"Shut up, Edward, if you know what's good for you!" She pointed at me. Edith always meant business when she pointed. Had a pet peeve about pointing at people.

"No! Edith, I am not going to shut up; tell me." I could see myself get up out of the chair and sort of tower over Edith, looking down at her face to face.

Edith scanned the room with her eyes, pointing at different objects. At one point, it looked like she was pointing at me. Not me the one that I was seeing, but me, the observer, in the dream. That gave me the chills, but I could tell that she had no idea of my presence, plus that would have been quite absurd.

"All this! Edward! Your awards, your books, and your trophies...All weren't entirely, If even at all due, to your work!" I was so mad at her at that moment. She had two husbands pissed.
"What do you mean, Edith?"

"You never gave credit where credit was due! Not to I! Not to John, and definitely not to Colin!" She was very mad, I could tell. I could see her practically spitting in my face.

"Oh, so you thought you would give credit for me with the open vase between your legs!?" I saw me smack her in the face and she fell to the ground.

I kind of felt sorry for Edith. I was very bad to her. Even seeing again the betrayal she had on me, I knew that all she wanted was love.

"I loved those men. What am I going to do without them?"

"Those men? Are you telling me you made love to John, too?" She looked away.

I told her that when I went to get that last book off of Colin's desk. I heard them giggling from the room in which I waited for her to leave. I thought nothing of it, but then I saw her re button her dress and I knew something was going on. I didn't know she had already told Colin to write a will like letter stating his death but after she left, I killed him.

"That's fine, Edward, I wanted the dickhead dead anyway. He wasn't that good in the sack!"

Edith picked up a trophy and came towards me.

"Let's see, Edward Larson, Author of Awe. Open your mouth, Edward. Let's see you say Aww!"

I thought this gesture was kind of confusing, but I thought she was acting silly, so I was going to act silly, too. I opened my mouth, and just like I would in a dentist chair, I said, "Aww."

That's when she did it. The old bitch shoved the tip of the trophy into my mouth and out the back of my head!

I couldn't believe my eyes. She just impaled me with my own trophy. I was for sure going to choke on my vomit if not in my dream. In real life, I knew I was probably in deep slumber there in the hotel room and probably in deep fermented Ghirardelli mocha cappuccino.

I was now placed right behind me in my dream, the tip of the golden pencil glistening with my blood and clots from my brain matter. I watch myself fall forward, helping the trophy further out the back of my head...I had to have been dead...and just as fast as I had beamed up behind me, I was back in the stadium of Dreamland where I had previously stood on the side of Edith and the other me and I watched in horror while Edith drug me outside and pulled the trophy out and threw me into the pool outside.

I awoke in a cold sweat...*was what I seeing the truth? Surely not, I'm not dead! How come I remember fighting with Edith that night now?*

I picked up the phone and on speed dial, I called Lily.

The phone rang.

"Hello?"

"Hello, sorry to bother you—"
"Just kidding I'm not able to answer the phone right now, please state your business after the tone!"

I got frustrated and slammed the cell shut turned around, thought about my dream a second. Thought of its calamity and then its silliness. Just thought it was my guilt. Am *I just seeing how Edith felt that night that I killed her?* I was so tired that I fell back to sleep.

I awoke the next morning by the light shining on my face through the flowered drapes on the windows. There I was again in the hotel room. Man, I had a busy day ahead of me. I turned to grab my briefcase, since Lily told me she had put the letter in my secret spot which was the bottom of the briefcase after I had taken the hard piece of plastic out, but then there it was again. The flowered purse.

When Albert came in, I pretended like I was still asleep.

"Ed, are you awake?" Al poked me in the arm.

"Oww!" He had poked me right where the IV was sticking me.

"What are you doing undressed again?" He stared down at my clothes on the floor.

"What do you mean?" I tried not to show him I knew what he was talking about and I really didn't. *What does he mean naked again?*

"Ed? Why did you put the IV back in? The pouch is empty." I looked up at the mistletoe pouch and for sure it was clear.

Albert sat down next to me and started stroking my leg. He probably would have gone under the covers if I would have let him.

"What the hell are you doing?" I jumped up naked. I didn't care. I grabbed my clothes and ran into the bathroom.

"I'm sorry Ed, I thought you just wanted to be freaky again," I heard him yell from the other side of the door.

"Get away from the door!" I looked around the bathroom and saw a cracked window.

"Ed, don't worry about what you did to Mr. Sivle. I forgive you. Just come back out here. You're just what the doctor ordered!"

I heard him yell that last nasty remark when I was halfway out the bathroom window right before I landed *smack* into the twigs and leaves below me.

I jumped into Al's still running Volkswagen when I saw Al standing at the doorway, dawning a come hither sign with his fingers on that perverted hand. There was no way in Hell that I was going to go back into that cabin. OH NO! And not only because he tried to put moves on me but I knew he was going to kill me since he knew what I did to his bird.

"Ed! What is that smell? Get out of my vehicle, Ed!" The last thing I remember is seeing Albert taking something out of his pocket, rolling it really tight and resting it in his mouth.

The next thing I knew there I was watching a screaming doctor running aimlessly around his yard with a bonfire of a house in the background. I put the vehicle in reverse and sped down the highway, back to Emerald Lake; back to the home that was going to imprison me but yet be my shelter for ten years.

When I got back to Emerald Lake, I found John out in the yard, raking up some leaves from the oak trees around the house. We didn't say much, he and I, but he did promise to board me up in the house, tell the town I went missing and he also promised to shop for me and bring me food every week. John did as he said. He was very loyal to me and for ten years that is how it stayed until the day I finally decided to be released into civilization yet again. The year two-thousand and four.

"Larson the Arson. Read all about it!" I was walking down the sidewalk to Marble Page Publishing with John.

"What is he talking about John?" I said coming up to the "City Crier".

"Nothing, Ed. It's okay now, it's in the past." I didn't want to take that for an answer so I paid the little loud mouth seventy-five cents and read the front page.

Larson The Arson Returns to Publics Eye:

Suspected Murderer and Well known author has been yet again suspected of causing millions of dollars damage to Dr. Albert Rigit's home in 94'. The inferno was set off by an unclosed stove burner that Larson had apparently left on, wanting to murder Rigit as Larson also did to their spouse and their father.

"They think I killed my father? But my father's not dead." I was getting really puzzled.

"Yes, he is. Ed, are you feeling okay? Let's go where we belong." He pointed up the stairs to the door that was decked with the sign: **M.P.P: Closed till Further Notice.**

"Closed? But why?"
"I closed it down after the funeral fiasco and haven't opened

it up since. The revenue the books have been bringing in a killer though. No pun intended." He smirked.

"What do you mean?" I glared at him.

"Nothing Ed, just a bad joke. It is what has let us keep the building though."

"Us?"

"Yeah, silly. Remember we own it?"

When we got inside, everything was in pristine order. Papers were in nice neat piles in cubicles around the building and computers were at each desk. I could not believe it. I was so happy to see the inside of M.P.P. again and a little more than before. Here I was, the co-owner of my grand estate with Jonathon Pricter, I didn't think the idea was that bad now.

"Here is your office and here is mine." He showed me two rooms with glass walls on one it read; **Ed Larson, Owner** and the second one read: **John Pricter, Editor.**

"Why does it say Editor?" I looked over at John. He was looking down.

"Because I think that all that you have been through, you deserve to be owner and I would be honored to be your editor again."

For the first time, John and I shook hands and I gave him all the credit he deserved since Edith wasn't there to do it for me.

Time went on as it always does, and John and I hired many an author. Some heard of me and some didn't. There were so many that came into my office to tell me that it was cool to work for Larson the Arson. None of them ever asked about my past. I didn't know whether it was because they already knew or they were told not to by John. Everything went well until the day John asked if he could retire. I told him it was okay, that we had our fun over the thirty-six years we had worked together. He told me he had found himself a replacement; her name was Lily Delano. He met her at some theatre production he was doing a book for and told her about us. She was twenty years younger than us and he was planning on marrying her, so I thought *What the Hell. John's been a loyal editor for me, what difference would it make for his fiancée to be editor? Ha, I laugh about it now but little did I know the impact this woman would have on my life...or should I say, death?*

I met Lily that day and she was already sharp and keen.

"Hello, Ms. Delano. I'm Ed Larson," I said with a sideways hand much older than the time I shook hands with Edith back when I was twenty-one.

"Just call me Lily." She smiled and returned my gesture.

"I hear you are quite a writer yourself. Maybe you should write a book along side me and then we can compare each other's thoughts." I asked.

"Oh, no, I don't really like to write that much. Just some plays here and there. I am a theatrical producer. I do costumes and makeup. Oh! and editing, of course."

"So, you have edited before right?" I was hoping John hadn't made a big mistake.

Yes, I have, from every revised play *Macbeth* to *the Sound of Music.*" It was an okay answer but not what I was looking for.

"That's good."

"I really loved all of the Larson literature I have read!"

"Oh, thank you. I am very appeased by that comment."

"But that last one *Behind Him*, that was a piece of crap!"

"I am sorry that you feel that way." That was the first time she had told me something good and then bad. That was Lily for you.
"Well, I am glad you took this job. I hope you and I will get along."

"Oh, I know we will...I'm just like a chip off the old block."

"What?" I was growing weary of everyone confusing me all the time.

"In other words I just came to work here because I wanted to be closer to the well known author of mystery! Ed!."

Two weeks into Lily being my editor, I still found myself at my desk writing short articles in the town paper, but not anything more...all the people that knew of my past were either dead or they just left it alone since charges of suspicion were dropped from me and the town was slowly eased back into the Larson

Lair. Then one day, Lily came up to me and told me to take a break. Take a breather, see if I could brainstorm my last masterpiece.

"Ed?" Lily laid the palms of her hands on my desk.

"Yes?" I looked up at her over my glasses. I could see in Lily's glasses an old piece of parchment paper of a man looking up at her.

I think it's time you take a vacation." She smiled at me.

"Yeah, I think that would be a great idea." I hadn't relaxed in awhile.

"Dammit, Ed, I'm just going to cut to the chase. John and I think you should retire." She moved out of the way and in my view now was John.

"You have one week, Ed." John said.

"I decided to hand the company over to Lily. You need to come and retire with me out on Emerald Lake."

"You can't hand the company over to her. I'm the owner."

"Standing yes, legally no. I received the whole company after you went missing."

I wanted to strangle this man for betrayal, but I guess he was right, plus my days of killing were over I was a changed man (more than I thought).

"I guess you're right."

"So, you go out to Emerald Lake with John, okay? and let me take care of this place for you." Lily chimed back into the conversation.

I said farewell and joined John back at Emerald Lake. Man, it was good to be home. A few days staying there, and one evening I was standing in the doorway overlooking the lake, and you know the rest of the story from there, but I will tell you what happened after that nightmare at the hotel.

I got out of bed. I didn't want to take one look behind me again, but I did and there was my briefcase and inside was a note that read:
Please if you love me, you will meet me at 202 Haight and Ashbury at two. I want to show you who I am. Eliana Larson

I grabbed a black suit out of the closet, combed my hair quickly and out the hotel room I went. I had already called a yellow hearse; the number was laying on the nightstand. The driver was the same one that I had left the day before.

"Where's my money?" he demanded. He wasn't moving.

"Here, just take me where I wanted to go yesterday." I threw money at him. I wanted to get on the move.

"Oh, I can't do that for you, place went up in smoke this morning."

"What do you mean up in smoke?"

"It exploded, flames shot in every direction I saw it!"

"Take me there anyway!"

"I wouldn't do that, it wouldn't look good for Larson the Arson to be there at the fire scene. Ha! That would be ironic."

"How do you know that name?"

"Everyone in San Francisco knows you, Ed. Everyone knew you were coming and I recognized you yesterday before you went screaming out of the cab."

I then thought that I was being a little absurd and too suspicious of everything and now I knew why Ol' Harold knew my name. I still wanted to go to Captain's Corner because Al Rigit's office was adjacent to the little restaurant. When we got there, I got out this time giving the cabbie his fare and he drove off, smiling.

"Now where is Rigit's place?" I said out loud.

A bystander must have heard me. "Rigit's place no longer exist sir, It went up in smoke along with Captain's Corner." A short stalking man shouted over the fire sirens.

"Just great." I thought. *The only person that could really diagnose me is probably little chunks of flesh like his feathered friend.*

I spun around a few times slowly just taken in the panoramic view, wondering if I could catch a glance of anyone: The yellow hearse, Lily, Ol' Harold and believe it or not at that moment I would have probably wanted to see Bloodsprayer and Edith too!.

Though I searched and searched I could not find a living or dead soul, one that I knew anyway.

What are you going to do now Ed?

I felt like my own psychiatrist, all I had been doing lately was asking questions about and to myself, I didn't need to do that that was what Sheriff Nick was for.

I slowly shook off the thoughts of anything remotely to do with anything, Hell I just couldn't take it anymore not the damn book not of what Bloodsprayer knew or what Dr. Rigit could tell me. All I wanted to do was to sit alone, sit alone and reminisce of Edith and I.

I found myself a bench a few blocks down from Captains Crumble, taking a seat I reached into the inner pocket of my P— Coat and pulled out my Ipod.

"The soundtrack of my life." I laughed to myself.

I turned it on and pressed my finger on the center round button and began to spin through the selections, that's all that was going on in my life just the constant spinning through selections of life.

I finally stopped at the song that described me the most I thought. Elvis Presley's version of Yesterday.

I sat back closed my eyes and listened I was only thirty six when I first heard this song done by Elvis the words didn't quite hit me back then as it had done now.

"Listen to this song hon." I said to Edith.

"What song is that Edward?" She said sarcastically but playfully.

"You know the song Yesterday?"

"Yeah "

"Well Elvis did his own version back in February." I felt like a little kid talking about his superhero.

"Yeah," Edith said very easily getting bored.

"Well, I'll just let you listen to it." I opened the record player lid and place the needle ever so carefully over the second set of grooves.

A scratchy sound began to play. I had listened to it a few times.

The king started the story of my life in which at the time I did not know.

"He doesn't know how right he is!" Edith and I said in unison.

We looked at each other and kind of smirked.

All three of us were singing now some of us out of pitch and tone.

The bench I was sitting on was cold.'

I must have been singing out loud.

"Yeah it did!" said a voice out of nowhere startled I dropped my Ipod and it turned off.

It was Officer Nick. *What the hell did he want now?*
"You seem a little distraught Ed, are you okay?"

I was close to tears. "I don't know that I am anymore."

Nick leaned up against me which made me feel very odd.

"You're a very beautiful person Ed that is what you are."

That made me feel a whole lot odder.

"Uhh thank you?" I looked at him confused.

"I think it's time you tell me the truth." Nick continued.

"What time is it?" I just remembered about the letter.

"It's about a quarter after nine, why?" He was as puzzled as I.
"Can you give me a ride to my apartment? I really need to get there as soon as possible!" I needed to get things done fast.

"Sure, Ed why not?" He pointed straight ahead to a gray 1987 Oldsmobile.

Man he's becoming a nuisance! Should I rid of him too? No! It's done with Ed your old and tired...You just need to tell him the truth, whether you spend the rest of your life in prison or walking these streets you will always be in your own prison.

We got in the car and the dash read: **Good Morning**

I laughed.

"What is it Ed?"

"Oh Nothing, it's just it's funny how back in eighty-seven you would have thought that your car telling you good morning was the coolest thing ever and nowadays the car could probably brush your darn teeth for you."

"Or dentures!"

"Hey!"

The ride to the hotel was quiet he must have not liked to talk or he took lessons from Edith.

"Would you like to come in?" I asked him when we got to the door.

"Sure why not?" All his answers seemed to come out this way.

I could have probably asked him "Do you think I killed Edith and Colin Louvaille and he would have probably would have replied "Sure why not?"

I turned on the lights in the room since I liked it to be dark in there I required dark curtains in my hotel rooms kept me calm and helped me write I would say...Ha

I went into the kitchen and grabbed two coffee mugs that I had just purchased from the Chinese man down in the Bart station right before I got on the first time.

When we sat down at the table I looked at Officer Nick looking at me the same way Al did back in Mona'me.

"What is it?" I didn't mean to but I felt myself blush.

Nick lifted the mug of chocolate to his lips and shrugged his shoulders.

"How did you know where to find me?"

"I wasn't actually out looking for you Ed." he laughed.

I stopped to think for a minute he was probably just checking out the explosion.

"I was just checking out the explosion." I was right.

"So why did you want to come here Ed?"

I went to my briefcase and pulled out the manilla folder that still held captured within it my life and that eerie bond I still had with the great beyond.

"I want to finish my book Nick and I want you to help me."

Nick seemed shocked that I had asked him of such a favor.

"Why me Ed?"
"It doesn't matter why Nick it just needs to happen!"

I wasn't mad at Nick or anyone really anymore, I just wanted it done.
The last couple of hours I tried to convince myself not to do it but there I was again, with those satanic thoughts.

"Well I don't know what to tell you Ed."

"What? are you trying to tell me that you won't allow me to write my book?"

After about two mugs of hot chocolate and a half an hour later Officer Nick was trying to hurry me along and I did not like that one bit.

"I'm not trying to be hasty Ed, it's just that I am not feeling that well that's all."

"Oh poor pig, probably just figuring out he's on his way to the slaughterhouse."
"Why don't you go lie down Nick? We don't have to leave for a few hours anyway and if your still not feeling well I'll drive."

"When did you learn how to drive?"

"You really aren't feeling good are you?"

I watched as Nick hobbled to the bed like a pet with a broken paw, swaying back and forth in a nauseated wind.

"You know what Ed?" Nick said softly.

"What is that Nick?" I said not breaking my concentration from the laptop.
There was nothing but the sound of silence, oh and the distant call of a traveler calling for a yellow hearse and the clinkety clang of my spoon as I sent little white skulls toward the bottom of a tainted chocolate in the cup that once belonged to a nosy cop.

As I reached for the bar of soap of the side of the shower I couldn't help but wonder what Officer Nick was going to say.

The hot water ran down my body, this was an all too familiar scene I washing away my crimes while there lie a dead corpse not even a hundred feet from me.

"Why has life been so complicated for me lately?"

The water was getting hotter it seemed.

I kept thinking about the events of the day and of the past.

The water was getting hotter!.

Ding Dong
"Oh shit I forgot Mr. Sonazuchi said there was something wrong with the pipes in my room and he was coming up to fix it."

"Mst. Rawson!" I heard the man call from outside the front door.

I couldn't wait for him to walk in and catch me red handed or red bodied thanks to the Hell of a shower.

I grabbed the suit I had lying over the toilet amd changed like Clark Kent in a phone booth.
"Only one way out!" *The fire escape!.*

As I headed toward the window I could hear the ever so fast but ever so slow turn of Mr. Sonazuchi's room key.

111

I was already running fast down the metal stairs that ran along the side of the building with the short little Asian got in the room.

I would have gotten down to Nick's Oldsmobile faster if I didn't have a mug in one hand and Nick's body flung over my shoulder.

I knew I couldn't just drop the dead body on the stairs without creating some suspicion so I dropped the mug the rest of the way down to the street watching it shatter into tiny jigsaw pieces.

Watching the mug shatter I wondered if my own body wold break if I fell the rest of the way down my cold escape.

When I got to the vehicle I laid Nick in the back seat and jumped in the driver seat starting the ignition and flooring it towards the Golden Gate.

This was it I thought finally the end of my masterpiece finished with no help from the bundle rolling around in the back seat.

I could see the Golden Gate from where I was at I couldn't figure out If I wanted to head back to Haight and Ashbury or see who it was that was my daughter.

"Your going to leave Ed and don't look back!" I said outloud to myself.

I stuck my Ipod's earphones in my ears and replayed from where I paused it earlier.

The song was just coming to a close.

"Why did you go Edith? Why!"

Wiping the tears out of my eyes I saw Edith one last time her eyes wet and looking at me in my rearview mirror, All of a sudden I couldn't remember how to drive anymore and went straight off the side of the bridge.

This time I didn't wake up in a hippie's shack or even in a hospital bed, No this time I was sitting in my hotel room next to Lily with my eyes fixed upon the television screen watching the news.

"Good Evening, the top story tonight an accident on the Golden Gate leaves commuters questioning the saftey of the bridges condition.

"Tonight?" I missed my meeting with my daughter."

I couldn't believe it.

A officer showed up on the screen.

"So far there has only been one body found and that was one of our own Sherriff James T. Nicolas."

"And they believe the other person who is not yet found is a woman?"

"Yes, The other person who's body still hasn't been found is that of Edith Larson."

"What!" My heart must have just stopped at his final words.

Lily turned off the television and just like a scene out of A Christmas Carol I was standing on a street watching a funeral progression.

The hearse stopped in from of me and John, Peter, Allison and Al Rigit took the coffin out of the back.

I watched as Lily walked past me not acknowledging me and towards the coffin where she proceeded to lift the lid.
"Good bye Mom."
I had never seen Lily's mom and was sorry I had not known about her death.
I walked up and saw the sight that brought new meaning to my life or should I say death.

Now I finally understood I was living Edith's life after she killed me, I must have been doing it for revenge or just to see how she was feeling the guilt and the secrets she was keeping.

Everytime I had seen her I was just seeing her reflection that is why I kept seeing her in reflective surfaces that is why people kept calling me Ma'am and why Al Rigit tried to come onto me back at the shack, I guess that also meant that Lily was my daughter.

Edith and I were inseperable even in death.

I couldn't take it anymore it was all just too much, I fainted and fell where I stood right there on Haight and Ashbury.

Everything went blank.

I felt a push at my shoulder.

"Edward, Edward honey are you asleep?" I could tell by her voice it was Edith.

"You must have fallen asleep trying to write." Edith said returning back downstairs.

I looked up and saw my computer screen there in front of me and to my right out the window was a frozen willow on the middle of a lake and while I gazed at the icicles coming off the rooftop I saw out of my peripheral vision John and Ally McKey's car pull into our driveway.

"Oh, that's right they were coming over for dinner so we could tell them the news."

"Edward!" I heard Edith call from downstairs.

"Yes, Edith?"

"I can't believe were going to have a baby! Oh she's either going to be a dream or the death of me!"

"Little do you know she might be both?" I said under my breath.

I looked at the computer screen in I deleted the jkksdhgk and the thousands of k's after that and began to type:

Prologue

As the clouds covered the sky, the wind began to howl between the trees.